For Mum and Dad – who always believed that I would write a book one day.

For Claire – my beautiful thoughtful wife who lost me for a month so that I could write this.

For Charlie and Lily – I hope you grow up believing anything is possible.

Love you all xx

To my wonderful Mum on her birthday, Love you!!

Steve xxx.

CHAPTER ONE

At 2.05am that morning Jacob Brooks was concentrating hard, beads of sweat glistening on his brow. He had already killed four people that morning and had identified his new victim. The man was in front of him, ten feet away, unaware of anyone approaching from behind. Stepping out of the shadows, Jacob brought up his gun, aimed it at the back of the man's head and fired.

The figure cried out, slumped forward onto the ground and lay still.

"Oh come on! That's not fair. I'm supposed to be on your side" said the 14 year old who lived in Canada.

Jacob chuckled to himself but it was picked up over the microphone headset he always wore while playing online Call of Duty.

"All's fair in love and war, my friend."

"What?"

"Never mind. Okay, I promise not to kill you again, let's go and ambush that troop to the north west and see if we can stock up on their ammo."

Even though Jacob had a full time job, he could never resist a quick go of this game in the evening and usually ended up battling it out online with random strangers. That was the beauty of the internet. He always tried to limit himself to just two hours but usually got so engrossed in the mission that he played on long into the night to the detriment of his mood and concentration the next day.

He controlled his character on the screen so that it ran along the fence, out of sight, until it got to the edge of a large encampment of enemy troops. He could see the guards that been posted along the camp and had a sudden urge to just run in there, all guns blazing. He stopped himself reasoning that he wouldn't get very far and he would lose his bonus.

Much better to wait until the guard changed in about twenty minutes, he knew he would be able to sneak in and get to the ammo store and back out without disturbing anyone. He found a large rock near the gatepost and made his character crouch down. Then he waited, taking off the headset and laying it beside him. The gentle flickering of the screen and the lateness of the hour eventually took its toll and ten minutes later, Jacob was softly asleep, snoring gently. A bead of saliva slipped from the corner of his mouth and ran down his cheek. Outside, the dark streets were still.

An hour later, his eyes flew open. Light streamed into his flat, a stunning white clear light that streamed through his windows and felt like someone was directing a searchlight into his flat. His first thought was that it was daylight but he glanced at his clock which showed 3.04am. Getting up gingerly, he absent-mindedly wiped away the dribble on his cheek with his sleeve and then shielded his eyes against the glare. He advanced towards the window. Dust particles twirled in the air and the sky outside was pure white and perfectly clear. A flock of birds, startled by the sudden change, flew up from their tree looking like tiny dots on a pure blank canvas. Then it was gone. The blackness returned so suddenly that Jacob stumbled backwards over his chair and landed on his back banging his head on the tiled floor.

He lay there, propped up on his elbows, trying to comprehend what had just happened. The glare of the light was still imprinted on his retinas and everything he looked at in the darkness was overlaid with a white circle. He blinked and rose slowly. His soldier was still on the screen crouching obediently behind a rock. Without thinking, he hit the power button on the console with his foot and turned the television off. He walked to the window. Had he dreamed what had just happened?

His answer lay in the streets. He lived halfway up a block of flats in the centre of Exeter and looking out now, he could see lights coming on in houses everywhere. People were coming out of their front doors in their pyjamas, hurriedly wrapping their dressing gowns around them and shivering in the cold night air. A dog was barking furiously, excited at the sudden unexpected appearance of its owner. This was not normal.

He went back inside and headed for the shower. He knew that he needed to get into work as fast as possible. If this was some unexplained phenomena that had happened across the country, possibly across the planet, then he expected a very busy day.

CHAPTER TWO

By the time Jacob had reached the Science and Future Research Station in Exeter, known globally as SFRS, it was indeed a busy place. Chief Brady was locked in his office with a team of experts, coming out only to walk pensively through the corridors of the large building. He managed to stretch his legs after the tension of the seemingly endless meetings he was enduring as well as checking in with other department heads along his circuitous route.

At 70 years old, and with 48 years in the field, he had earned respect and reverence from his staff and worked them hard. He expected the best from his staff and made sure that each and every trainee he recruited from universities were the best at what they did. Consequently, the SFRS was world renowned. It specialised in "everything from the clouds upwards" as Brady tried to explain it to new potential investors. The earth was for geologists - he preferred to look at the stars. At this sprawling building they analysed the atmosphere, kept track of comets, watched the sun patiently for solar flare patterns, tracked the stars they knew and did everything they could to find new ones.

Over the last few years, there had been plenty for Brady and his staff to get excited about. A new cluster of stars had been identified that had previously been blocked from view by Jupiter before a new satellite mounted telescope opened their eyes to new possibilities. There had also been a comet that seemed to be heading straight towards Earth for a couple of months but once it was within 50 or so light years away, the alarm faded away. It was going to miss by a long distance, much to everyone's relief. The comet hadn't made the news, of course, that was one of the SFRS' little secrets. There were some things the general public didn't need to know and as they had the biggest and best telescopes in the world, they were always going to get the news on these things first.

The glare on March 7th though couldn't be hidden from anyone. Most of the 7 billion people on the planet saw it. If you were awake, it almost blinded you, whiting out your vision like a snowstorm and when it left 35 seconds later, it left a retina burn that lasted much longer. It left an after image of myriad reds and blues that span round your vision. Apart from this, no ill effects seem to have been reported. If you were asleep, it generally woke you up. Imagine being in a deep sleep, then someone turning on the brightest light you've ever seen two inches from your eyeballs. It even seemed to permeate inside buildings. The only people that seemed to escape the light were in a coma, or heavy sleeping tablets. But those who awoke to the confusion were just as scared now as the ones who had lived it.

It was Brady's job, in part, to reassure the public on these matters. He was the public figurehead to calm public fears and to explain the science behind the drama. Comets will almost certainly miss every time. The suns solar flares followed a pattern, and even though it may knock out your satnav for a short while, everything was fine. The glare though scared Brady as much as anyone. He had never see anything like it, no one had. And what's more, he had no idea, NO idea what on earth could have caused it. His calm statement on the news earlier was the best bluff he could think of in the time had available to him and he knew that although there wouldn't be a single scientist that would agree with him, none of them would break rank and offer some other solid theory that made sense. There were no other theories that made sense.

His walk round the departments this time ended with the unpleasantness of Konrad Kaden, the head of waveforms and magnetism. Brady was always excited by science but even he struggled to keep up with the findings of this particular group. Kaden came up with a few good ideas here and there but he was an irritating man to most who knew him. Overweight and usually bad tempered, he had few social skills but was good at his job and caused Brady few problems.

Chief Brady knocked on Kaden's glass door that led to his office. He watched as the man scowled to himself, turning slowly in his leather chair before attempting a smile as he saw who it was that was disturbing him from his work. As he got to his feet and began to come towards the door, running fingers through his lank greasy hair as he went, Brady surveyed the scene behind the approaching man. There were two people in Kaden's department. He could see Rebecca Smith now, white coat and goggles on, peering dutifully into a microscope at something. She was a good worker and often seemed eager to impress. She was tall and slim and quick with a joke if the situation required it but very committed to her work. She reminded him of his first wife back in the seventies – the same perfect blue eyes and long wavy hair that framed her face. Brady made a mental note to reread her CV when all this nonsense was over. Jacob Brooks was the other. He remembered hiring this guy 5 years ago but hadn't heard Kaden mention him much since. He always seemed to be here, late night and early mornings but never came up with anything that had excited anyone so far. He supposed every organisation had to have their plodders, their workhorses, but he had expected so much more from Jacob. His results from university had been exemplary, his CV impressive but he remembered the light of excitement in Jacob's eyes at the interview and that had convinced Brady to hire him. He remembered that sparkle from his own eyes when he was Jacobs age. Now the fire in those brown eyes had seemed to go out and he seemed to look older than his twenty six years.

Konrad Kaden opened the door. He was a large man and seemed to fill the doorframe. His greying hair was swept back away from his forehead and slicked back with a handful of grease every morning before being tied into a ponytail at the back. He smiled at his boss, showing his yellowing nicotine stained teeth.

"Good morning Alfred. How are things going in there?" Konrad enquired in his soft Polish accent. "Any breakthroughs? Is there anything I can do to help?"

"Nothing so far Konrad. The situation is the same as I messaged out to everyone twenty minutes ago. The light seems to come from everywhere all at once. There's no spike of irradium levels which is what I'd expect for that much light, and there's no heat to go with it. Have you got any more readings from the magnesium meter? That can at least show us if the Radon counter is working correctly."

Konrad shook his head and his ponytail swished behind him. "I have readings but nothing out of the ordinary. I had an idea that it could well be a reflected glare from another sun. Something elsewhere, just outside our solar system that is so big, a solar flare would ricochet into our viewpoint if it's done at just the right angle. I mean it's a vague idea and I've only just thought of it but what do you think?"

Brady looked impressed. "It's certainly a possibility, I'll mention that to the other chiefs, stick on the pile on possibles and probables. To be honest, at the moment, most things sound improbable but we have no other ways forward. I think the general public are calming down though. There doesn't seem to be any after effects as far as we can see. Well done though, keep thinking those shiny thoughts and let me know of any more." He glanced at Jacob. "And see if you can get the rest of your team up to scratch too. I'll leave it to you then."

In Konrad's department, there was only room for the three staff. Large computers and screens were set up across the desks, the walls lined with posters of waveforms and calculations. A large electronic blackboard was set up on one side showing the latest workings of the team, including the solar flare idea and small looping writing. A giant computer screen was scrolling down figures from readings collected throughout the building, streamed to all departments constantly.

The building itself was the largest in the country. It had been set up in the 1950s - that decade where the world thought that aliens were everywhere and endlessly wrote and made films about them. The government had set aside a sizable part of its budget to finance the building of a new centre that would investigate the possibility of life in outer space. This expanded over the years to its current remit. The decor, however, was still straight out of the fifties. Scientists were not known for their attention to furnishings and everything was painted in grey and black. Whenever it was deemed that a redecoration should happen then the contractors were asked to get the same paint out of the cupboard and repaint the whole building in the same colours all over again.

Rebecca was still peering into her microscope, lost for the moment in her macrobiotic world of bacteria samples. Jacob, however, was staring at Konrad, open mouthed. They had been working on the solar flare idea all morning. The idea had come to Jacob when he was driving blearily into work a few hours earlier. When he had checked in, he had gone straight to Konrad, his superior, and explained it to him. The older man had listened intently and suggested that Jacob work his theory up a little more using the equipment in the office. Now he had stolen the idea for his own. Red spots of fury were appearing on his cheeks, but he kept silent. What was the point in saying anything? He had heard this all before many times.

Konrad looked at him, amused, wiping his hand through his hair again, brushing a few greasy strands away from his piggy eyes. "Not happy again Jacob? What is it this time? You're getting more miserable every day recently. Is it Rebecca again? Is she still refusing to go out with you, you two little lovebirds?" He grinned, a malicious smile that didn't touch his flat grey eyes.

At the sound of her name, Rebecca looked up from her microscope and smiled coolly at Konrad.

"Konrad, you know very well that Jacob is most likely furious that you just took credit for his idea that he had spent the last few hours on. And I don't blame him. You could have at least given him a mention, seeing as though he brought it to you in good faith. You did the same thing last week." Her blue eyes started at him coolly and Konrad was, as always, struck by her beauty.

Jacob looked away, embarrassed.

"I am in the room Rebecca", he muttered, but shot her a thankful glance anyway. Rebecca flashed him a smile and returned to her work, her red hair tumbling down once more around the microscope.

"Jacob, we work as part of a team, you know that. When – or should I say if – you ever make your way up the ladder to my position, then you can put forward your teams ideas like I do. Alfred will not want to bother with people in your role. That is why he makes people like me heads of department"

He came close to Jacob now and whispered in his ear. Jacob could smell stale cigarettes on his putrid breath.

"And you are not good enough for my role, you know that. A couple of passable ideas here and there will not get you noticed here. Get me my results on the radiation levels by noon".

Jacob sighed, the hopelessness overwhelming him again. He was used to Konrad's ways of course but the frustration still bubbled away, even more so now when there was an actual event happening and people needed answers. He was already been in and working when Rebecca had arrived that morning, her greeting smile taking his breath away as it always did. She was as committed to the job as he was, thriving on their figures and getting her thrills from positive results. They always worked well together, her analytic brain and fierce intelligence complimenting his way of thinking outside the box and dedication.

Jacob had thought often about asking her out for dinner outside of work but could never quite bring himself to do it. He enjoyed their time together at work too much to spoil it with awkwardness. And although he knew she viewed him as a good friend, there was never any flirting between them. She wasn't that type of person. If she was interested, she would let him know, it was very black or white sometimes with Rebecca.

On top of that, he knew she regarded him as weak when it came to dealing with Konrad. He had never been able to deal with the blatant copying of his ideas and the obvious way that he belittled Jacob at any given opportunity. He tried to stand up for himself but could never quite summon up the courage. He did when he first started the job but after a few instances at the beginning of his career, his will ebbed away and now he was left as a husk of his former self, still able to think outside the box, still able to formulate brilliant ideas but unable to follow it through to claim them as his own. His cheeks burned as he stared at Konrad's retreating back.

CHAPTER THREE

Texas, USA.

The Westward Old Peoples Home in downtown Texas was one of the more downtrodden homes in the area. It had barely passed its annual inspection last summer and was managed by a disinterested Mrs Abel Loritz. She spent most of her days now locked away in her office chain smoking and talking to her sister in Illinois. When her staff really needed her, she sighed heavily, lifted her giant bulk steadily out of her reclining leather chair and saw to matters as quickly as possible. The staff could run the home by themselves and preferred it when Mrs Loritz was in her office. As long as they got paid, they were happy to look after the residents with minimal assistance from the manager.

At ten past four in the afternoon of March 8th, Raymond, a long serving orderly had cause to visit the smoke filled office to sign for the key to the medicine cabinet. After minimal communication from Mrs Loritz and a scowl when he had asked to leave ten minutes earlier, Raymond beat a hasty retreat. He was halfway down the corridor, breathing in clean air again when he realised he had left his clipboard on her desk. With a heavy sigh, he returned to the office and knocked softly. When he received no reply, he pushed the door open and began an apology for disturbing her.

A cigarette was still glowing gently on the desk. The telephone was hanging by its cord and the orderly could hear the dial tone. Of Mrs Loritz, however, there was no sign.

Belfast, Northern Ireland

Marlene Lewis opened the farm gate and strolled down to the lower field carrying a sandwich and mug of strong tea. Her husband had called her and asked her for his daily favour five minutes ago. Marlene and Mark had been married for twenty three years and Mark had been making this joke daily for at least the last fifteen. The small innuendo never failed to bring a warm smile to his wife's lips though and she was always pleased to spend some time with him as he broke for lunch. The day was bright, the wind gentle and Marlene could see her husband look up from his work as she approached, raise a hand in greeting and smile at her.

He had been treating a sheep with a sore foot, his simple medicine box at his feet. He was crouched in the dirt, one knee pressed into the mud and he returned his hand now to settle the sheep he was holding. She was thirty yards away when she glanced sideways at a gambolling lamb. When she looked back, her husband was gone. The sheep he had been holding bleated and ran back towards its flock, limping slightly.

The mug fell limp in Marlene's hands as she gasped in shock and the tea destined for her missing husband spilled out and soaked into the earth.

La Rochelle, France

Jacques rubbed his eyes in tiredness and blinked trying to concentrate on the road ahead. He steered his truck back into the right hand lane and brought the speed back to 60. The last thing he wanted was to get pulled over by some over eager gendarme. He had been on the road since midnight and should really take a break but he was on a deadline and got a nice healthy bonus if he managed to get his delivery to the factory in Rouen before 8am. That bonus would pay for repairs on his sons motocross bike and that was worth losing a little sleep over. They spent most weekends on the motocross track near their simple home and he had found that the most pleasure he gained nowadays was watching his son enjoy his hobby.

Luckily, he had been on a small break when the white light had come. It had blinded him temporarily, lighting up his cab where he sat with a steaming cup of coffee in his hands. He dreaded to think what would have happened if he had been driving and once he had set off again had actually seen a few accidents being attended to along his route. He was listening to the radio now, the excited chatter of experts giving their formulated opinions.

He glanced at a road sign to his right. 43km to Rouen. He could make that without stopping again, he was sure of it. He pressed a button on the radio and his CD started playing, he twisted the volume and started singing along, trying to clear the exhaustion from his brain.

Then he vanished.

The truck rumbled on, cab empty, stereo blaring. After two miles, the road gently curved to the east and Jacques' vehicle carried straight on, slamming against the barriers at the side of the road. It shuddered, and came to a halt while cars sped past blaring their horns.

CHAPTER FOUR

March 13th 20.30 GMT

Jacob rubbed his tired eyes and looked across at Rebecca. They had finished for the day and handed their results into the central team for further investigation. They would have stayed longer but exhaustion had finally taken its toll and they admitted defeat; their empty stomachs rumbling louder and louder as the evening progressed.

"Okay", he said, drumming his fingers on the steering wheel impatiently and keeping one eye on the brake lights of the car in front. "We've narrowed it down to 7 things. So we're getting there. I think"

"I can't help it. It's all so ..nice!"

"It's fast food! None of its nice, it just wants you to think that." He grinned. "Would you like me to show you a video of the way they make burgers? With the orange gloop? Would that help?"

Rebecca stuck her tongue out at him and did that cute nose wrinkling thing that he liked so much. Well, that on its own was worth all the stress of waiting for her decision, he thought.

"You know," she said, going off on a tangent "I really wish you'd stand up to Konrad. He's an idiot. And you are not. And you let him walk all over you, it really annoys me."

"I will, I will. It's just...tricky that's all. He's my boss. And you know I need this job. My crappy one bedroom flat won't pay its own rent will it?"

"Yeah but the ideas you have sometimes. I don't know where they come from, you come from it from a completely different angle than most of us, some weird angle and it does his head in everytime. It really gets to him, you know. That's why he he's so mean to you, you know. He knows you can do his job."

Jacob had heard this little rant before, usually waiting for their after work burgers and he always had the same strange mix of humiliation and excitement that she was defending him.

"Yeah but my last idea about the solar flare from another sun was rubbish, glad he got that one."

"Not the point I was making" She turned her attention back to the garish food menu.

"Okay!", she clapped her hands together. "Let's go for ...that chicken thing. No, two chicken things and a coke. And fries. And onion rings. Oh god, I love onion rings. It's been a long day Jacob my friend and those onion rings are dancing in front of my eyes"

"Okay, mad lady. Your wish is my whatever. Oh thank God, at last, here we go"

He drove up to the now vacant speaker stand.

"Whopsters - Where your everyday food needs are catered for in a fast and friendly manner. Can I take your order please?" said a disembodied male voice. As with all these machines, the voice was just on the lower level of being able to hear and Jacob leaned slightly out the car window making him wonder, not for the first time, why they continued to come to these places after work.

"Hi, erm...2 chicken platters please, 2 cokes, 2 fries.."

"Onion rings" Rebecca hissed.

"I know! Yeah, er, onion rings. And that's it I think. Do we get a gift?"

"Are you under 12 Sir?" said the voice.

"Yes. And driving."

"As I have reason to believe you may be over 12 Sir, you can purchase a free gift for £2 at the window if you may. Or provide documentary evidence to the contrary. We do have an offer on today of...."

A silence. Jacob stretched out of his car a little further to hear his next words above the idling engines next to him, also ordering.

"Yes? An offer of?"

From the speaker next to his ear came screams. Hard and harsh in Jacob's ear, he recoiled.

"What the.." That was an older male voice in the speaker. Jacob looked across at Rebecca, puzzlement in his eyes.

"Hello? Are you still there?" he shouted into the microphone. "Okay, fine. Great service as always. Thank you!" He put the car into gear and drove slowly forward to the window.

As they drew up, they surveyed the scene. A man with bushy eyebrows and a badge stating "Derek. Shift Manager. Here to Help" printed on it above 5 stars was looking dumbfounded, staring at the space where an assistant should be seated.

"He was here" he said in a quiet voice, looking at Jacob but not really seeing him. "I was looking at him and he was here. Then he just...wasn't." He blinked and licked his lips. "Damn" he finished. He slammed the little window shut and Jacob sat back in his seat.

"Friendly. Real five star service there then", he said.

They relocated to the local fish and chip shop down the road instead. Inside, seated next to a small table laden with the usual slimy tomato sauce bottle and crusty salt and pepper, Rebecca was waving a chip thoughtfully at Jacob.

"That was weird." She said. "Dead weird. Maybe he jumped out of the window."

"We would have seen him" said Jacob. "I was looking at the window. And that guy was looking at him. You know Michael Stipe is missing, don't you?"

Rebecca looked at him, startled by the sudden change in conversation.

"Who?"

"Michael Stipe? R.E.M.? Lead singer? Or was anyway. They split up a few years ago. Anyway, the point it, he went missing from his house yesterday. He was supposed to be at a meeting or something, didn't turn up. Same with that Cuba bloke."

"I'm sorry. A bloke from Cuba?"

"No, not a bloke from Cuba. Cuba something something. Hang on". He got his phone out and quickly searched for 'missing Cuba', his spare hand absent-mindedly grabbing more chips. "Here we go, Cube Gooding Jr, film star. Disappeared from the film set a couple of days ago. Blah blah, blah, wife is puzzled, no reason for him to run away, had everything to live for. It was his birthday apparently."

"Maybe he couldn't hack getting older. Was it a big landmark one?"

Jacob searched again, noting with displeasure that he was getting his phone screen greasy with his chip smeared fingers.

"46. Nothing special. Weird"

"So you're linking the R.E.M. guy, the American actor guy and the bloke from the burger place and coming up with...?"

A headache was what he had and it was pounding. But this was good. All his good ideas seem to come accompanied with a headache. There was something obvious here that he was missing.

"You think this is linked in with the white light?" Rebecca said, spearing a piece of scampi with her fork.

"No idea. I just know we always got taught never to discount the impossible or improbable. There's always an answer out there for everything, it's just finding it. And sometimes that answer turns out to be plain weird."

As Rebecca watched him, he fiddled with his phone, flicking it on and off absently, deep in thought. His eyes seemed so far away to her, his mind somewhere connecting dots, solving problems.

He looked at her, a glint in his eyes.

"Hey, if we're talking plain weird then you know who we need to call."

She smiled, the sparkle now in her eyes.

"Barry" they said together.

CHAPTER FIVE

"Jacob, my friend!" Barry called out.

They were alone in the fish and chip shop now and Jacob had his phone on speaker. Rebecca grinned widely, it always amused her that Jacob's old friend lived in Australia and had the plummiest English accent you could find. She always expected him to say Toodle Pip at the end of every conversation.

"Hey Barry", Jacob said. "How's it going mate?"

"Perfect thank you, and I'm hearing you loud and clear. Loving this technology nowadays. How's work? And how's that beautiful Rebecca of yours?"

Jacob flushed red in an instant.

"Barry, she's not..."

"Hi Barry" said Rebecca, cutting in. "How's sunny Melbourne? When are you going to invite us over?"

"Ah Rebecca, you know you can come over anytime you like my dear. I will pay for the finest seat for you. Jacob can get his own ticket."

Jacob grinned. He and Barry had studied at university together, rooming and studying hard together. They had found a common friendship in the puzzles of science and the mysteries of the universe. Also in inventing ice cream. When they weren't studying, they had experimented with hundreds of flavours, from vodka and blueberries to the legendary gerbil muesli and strawberries. It had done so well, they had briefly thought of giving up all their studies to start their own business but in the end common sense prevailed and their love of science had won.

Barry had been headhunted for a job in Melbourne, heading up a science lab researching the effects of GM foods and Jacob had joined the SFRS.

Barry's career had bloomed with huge pay rises and responsibilities whereas Jacobs had stalled at the first hurdle, stuck under the imposing shadow of Konrad. They had stayed firm friends, however, and often spoke for many hours on Skype debating new scientific theories.

"Barry mate, have you noticed anything weird over there?" Jacob said.

"Apart from the weird bright light you mean?

"Yeah I think that one's fairly well covered thanks. No, I mean anything else that just doesn't make sense." He didn't want to lead Barry on this, it always works better if two brains are thinking things through themselves and hopefully coming to the same conclusions.

"Well, the temperature's damn hot even for January. And my car is making a weird clanking noise."

"How is that weird?"

"Because my neighbour is getting exactly the same clanking noise, that's why. Thinking about it, I'm not entirely sure that's the groundbreaking story you're after. The only big news round here at the moment is Mel Gibson quitting his latest film. He hasn't turned up for work for a couple of days. There's rumours he's run off with Megan Fox, his co-star. Listen I've got to go mate. It might be evening for you, but I'm at work now and I've got important people waiting to suck up to me. Give me a ring tonight, tomorrow morning whatever." The line went dead.

"So where does that get us?" Rebecca asked, mopping up the last of her tomato sauce with a chip. "Apart from confirming that Megan Fox is not to be trusted."

"Well, it tells us to look outside the box. It tells us that things are a little weird and that lots of little weird things might turn out to be one big weird thing."

"Or alternatively it's just you that's weird and you need some sleep".

"Probably the latter", Jacob agreed, "come on, I'll drive you home."

CHAPTER SIX

Jacob woke, stretched and got out of bed slowly. He always showered with the radio on blasting rock music as loud as he could to try and kick start his brain but today he stood there silent as the water coursed over him. He had had a dream and was trying desperately to keep hold of the fragments. Something about Michael Stipe and the burger place. Something that didn't make sense. He dried himself off, dressed, grabbed his phoned and checked his Facebook.

It's Penny's birthday today. Wish her a happy birthday by leaving her a message he was prompted. Something clicked inside his mind, the neural connections firing even at this early hour and he ran to his car, eyes wide.

It usually took him thirty minutes to get to work but he put his foot down and risked being caught by the speed cameras along the way. He had to speak to Rebecca.

Chief Brady was waiting for him when he got there.

"Brooks. We need to talk, sort your gear out, grab a coffee and meet me in my office 2 minutes. Rebecca's already there."

Rebecca in already? That was unusual. She was as keen as he was with science but he always beat her in.

Three and a half minutes later, he was seated in one of Brady's expensive leather chairs facing him across the desk. Rebecca was next to him, looking just as confused as he was.

Brady got straight to the point.

"Konrad hasn't turned up for work. He hasn't called in sick and it's definitely not a holiday day. There isn't any time off allowed anyway as you know as I've cancelled everybody's till we figure out this great light thing. I had my receptionist drive by on the way in and he's not answering his door either. Anyway, that's not your problem, that's mine. The point is, I've got no-one to supervise you two and Konrad is the idea guy."

Rebecca opened her mouth to speak but Brady held up his hand and continued.

"Your department is great at what it does but at the moment I need things to happen quicker elsewhere. I need to get a lead on this white light and the astrophysics unit need as much help as possible so I'm closing you down until Konrad gets back and you can work with Jerry here."

For the first time, Jacob noticed a figure behind him, standing in the doorway. He's never seen him before but that was not unusual. A great many people worked at the SFRS behind a great many closed doors and hidden offices. He was very thin, very pale and he gave them a brief cold smile before turning back to Brady.

"He'll look after you and show you what he needs. Close your experiments down for now and work hard for this man"

Jacob almost got up to go with Jerry but then sat back down. His cheeks reddened and he swallowed hard.

"Chief, I have an idea." he started.

"Sorry son, I haven't got time for your ideas. I need to get going with this new test. The light didn't emit any heat but that doesn't necessarily mean it.."

"Sir, please let me try something first. When's Konrad's birthday? I have no idea. He's never said anything before, never brought in cakes.."

"Cakes?" Brady spluttered, "Why the hell are we now talking about cakes? Brooks, I need your support on this one, I need you to get in gear and help me, for Gods sake"

"I know, I know but it's an idea I've got" Jacob persisted, "Konrad's missing right? And so is the guy from the burger place. And I'm sure it was his birthday. I'm sure of it. Rebecca, can you remember?" He was gabbling now, desperate to get his point across.

He turned to Rebecca who was staring at him with confused eyes.

"Jacob, shouldn't we.."

"He had a badge! Remember? Two badges actually. Next to his work one was a happy birthday badge. Then – he – disappeared."

Brady half stood up.

"What the hell are you talking about?" he shouted.

"R.E.M.!" Jacob replied, his voice now an octave higher. His shirt was stuck to his back and he could see Rebecca out of the corner of his eye looking at the floor in embarrassment. "Michael Stipe. You know, Losing My Religion? You must know. Jerry?"

He turned in his chair to face the thin man who was looking at him with a mix of amusement and concern.

"That's me in the corner. You know the guy?" Jacob pleaded.

Chief Brady had had enough.

"Okay Brooks. Get out."

"What?" Jacob said. He had never been in trouble before, not even at school and he wasn't entirely sure how he'd got himself into this situation.

"I said get out. I've just told you I need help. Right now, I've got a hundred journalists ringing me every hour. I've got secretaries of state ringing me for updates and now I've got crucial members of staff going awol on me. What I don't need is some upstart rambling about birthdays. Now get out, go home, take the rest of the week off and come back when you can focus on what needs to be done."

He stared at Jacob, unblinking.

Jacob looked across at Rebecca but she was refusing to look back. She would always try and back him up with Konrad but there was no way she was going to go against the chief. She valued her job too much.

Jacob stood up. He went to speak but again the hand came up from Brady and his expression made it clear the conversation was over.

CHAPTER SEVEN

At the upper reaches of the atmosphere, 5 miles above the Earth, three giant crafts hovered. They were impossibly huge, dwarfing the planet below. If you looked at them directly, as the astronauts in the International Space Station had done occasionally, you would look straight through them. The telescopes trained on the stars from Earth could still see their beloved constellations and comets beyond them.

But they were there.

The black heavy forms of their ships flickered dimly and strengthened as power coursed through them. A single beam of light shot continuously from each ship, connecting to each other and encircling the planet. Another larger beam of yellow diffused light came from the underside of each ship and shone down on the continents below. Within this light, dozens of tiny specks floated upwards lazily towards each craft in large groups and as each collection of specks reached its destination, they seemed to melt into the ship, connecting with the giant object in a small pinprick of red and sending a ripple through the pendulous form as if it were water.

Within the ships, dark shadows moved. The harvest had begun.

CHAPTER EIGHT

Jacob lay on his back on his bed, screwed his hands into fists and punched downwards hitting the duvet hard. How stupid could he be? He loved his job, lived for it and he should be there right now helping out, being a team player.

His mind, usually so clear, was a mess. It whirled with the humiliation of being ordered home from work and the confusion of the white light, the missing people. He'd made connections in his brain but they didn't make sense to him and, quite obviously, not to anyone else either. He knew something was wrong and part of his brain was happy to accept this, happy to investigate this and run with any mad theory that Jacob was coming up with. But it seemed the scientific part of his brain was on lockdown, refusing to believe what he was proposing.

He knew about the white light. Nobody had figured out what it was, why it did what it did and where it had come from. But maybe that was the point – it had come *from* somewhere. And then there were the missing people. Now, he knew that people went missing all the time. Some had run away, some had been killed, some came back from wherever they had been. People sometimes need an escape. God knows, Jacob felt exactly the same way at the moment. It had crossed his mind earlier to pack up his stuff and drive – somewhere. He wasn't sure he could face going back to work and facing his colleagues.

But this seemed different. People were disappearing on the spot. The guy in the burger place. Michael Stipe. There was another story in the paper today of the deputy mayor of some town a few miles from where he lived who had missed the most crucial meeting of his career and people couldn't understand why. And another seemingly innocuous story of the centre forward for Brentwood FC who hadn't turned up for training that week and was being fined for misconduct. He would lose his place in the team if he didn't contact the club by Saturday but so far they hadn't heard anything. The transfer window was coming up and the paper was speculating that he was trying to make a statement and get other clubs interested. If so, it wasn't working, said the club chairman.

These stories and experiences seemed to be melting into one in Jacobs head but he still didn't understand why. He put his pillow over his head and lay there, listening to the sound of his own breathing and then screamed in frustration into the soft material.

"Your day not getting any better then?"

He whipped off the pillow to see Rebecca standing there, unable to conceal the amusement on her face.

"What? How did you..?"

"The door was open, you lummox. What is wrong with you? Are you okay?"

Jacob was suddenly aware that Rebecca was in his flat. Next to his bed. She had never been into his flat before and he flushed red again. This was something that she noticed straightaway and smiled again.

"You know, I couldn't have pictured this better if I'd tried. If I had to describe the flat of a single twenty something scientist, then I think I would have been spot on."

His eyes took in yesterday's clothes strewn across his un-vacuumed floor, the dishes from the last two meals still on the drainer waiting to be washed up and the pizza box on top of the TV in the corner where it had been for at least a week now. He had never really had a reason to clear up properly, nobody ever visited him and his family were all up north. If any visiting were to be done for special family occasions then he went up there. He had a 6 monthly tidy up for the landlord but that had been three months ago and the flat was in full squalor mode. He also noticed with a lurching feeling in his stomach that amongst the posters of atoms and periodic table on his walls were several print outs of Holly Willoughby that he had downloaded from the internet. Oh, and yesterdays pants that were next to the bedpost and perilously close to Rebecca's right foot.

"Sorry 'bout the mess", he mumbled and sat up on his bed, tossing the pillow aside. Rebecca took the opportunity to sit down on the end of the bed and Jacobs mind seemed to scramble and all he could hear himself thinking was "She's on my bed! She's on my bed!" Pathetic. He really needed to get his head clear here before he embarrassed himself completely.

"So what happened today Jacob? The Chief was absolutely fuming after you went, he started talking about getting rid of you and asking me for ideas for replacements."

"Oh God. I'm so sorry. What did you say? "

"I told him the lady who cleans the vending machines was a perfect replacement and she had some startling ideas on proton replacement therapy for enzyme fuel processors. What do you think, you muppet?"

She reached over and placed her hand on his, gave it a gentle squeeze. His mind scrambled again.

"I told him you were the best scientist of your age that I've ever come across and he should give you another chance." She patted his hand again and returned it to her lap.

"But I also told him I had no idea what you were talking about and I thought you were ill. He was fine by the end of the day, distracted by the white light saga and another round of meetings. Konrad didn't turn up all day and the Chief's happy to keep our department closed down. He's done the same with a few non-essential departments and we're all on white light duty in the main processing unit. Boring as hell and no one's getting anywhere but needs must."

Jacob looked at her, his eyes moist.

"Thanks Rebecca. Thanks for standing up for me, God I know I made a complete fool of myself today but my head is just spinning. I don't know whether I'm mad or stupid or both. I've had the occasional mad idea here and there, you know I have. But I've never been so confused and stressed as I am now." He held his head in his hands and sighed, his breath ragged as he tried to keep his composure.

She clapped her hands together and shifted her weight so she faced him.

"Okay, scientist boy, tell me everything. No, actually scrap that. Get me a drink and then tell me everything. Start at the start, tell me all the bits that make sense, all the stupid bits and then let's see if we can make anything scientific or otherwise out of this."

For the next fifteen minutes, he told her everything he could think of. Skipping quickly over the white light – they both knew all there was to know about that one – he reminded her of the burger place guy, the missing celebrities, the story he'd seen about Mel Gibson and the footballer not turning up. As he was explaining it, he knew it sounded stupid but something inside him was telling him not to give up on it.

"Okay" Rebecca said, "So I get the idea that people are supposedly going missing. But what's that got to do with anything? How does that tie in with the white light?"

Before he could answer, his mobile rang. It made them both jump with its loudness.

"Barry? How you doing mate?" Jacob said.

"Lovely but a bit freaked out Jacob my old friend, and that's lovely with a small L and freaked with a capital F" said Barry, his voice ringing clear across the thousands of miles. "I've been thinking about what you asked me. About whether there was anything weird going on over here. Apart from the usual Australian behaviour."

"Okay", Jacob said slowly, "and..."

"Well, you remember me saying about Mel Gibson. And my neighbour with the car? With the clanking noise?"

"Yeah"

"Well, I went to his birthday party today. Lovely little soiree it should have been. Barbecue, wine on the veranda and chat long into the night. But it all ended after an hour."

"Why?" Jacob said. Rebecca leaned in to try and catch what Barry was saying and her perfume filled his senses. He tried to concentrate on the phone call.

"It ended with my lovely neighbour telling a really boring story about fixing his car and how he was certain the mechanic was ripping him off. He's got a Ford Mustang and apparently it's known to have some kind of fault which affects all Mustangs. He looked it up on the internet for goodness sakes – I mean, who does that? Anyway, I never found out what happened in the end – just as he was telling me about the exhaust system, he...disappeared. Right in front of me."

There was silence on both ends of the line. Ten thousand miles of space between them crackled slightly. As freaky as this was for Barry, it suddenly left Jacob with a serene sense of calm as if the rough sea in his brain had become a garden pond, free from ripples.

"Jacob mate, are you still there?"

"Hmmph"

"The whole place went nuts. It wasn't just me he was telling the story too, his wife was there bringing round drinks and rolling her eyes at people when they caught hers, she wanted him to finish his boring story and help with the party but couldn't get his attention. There was at least three other people sat round me listening to this guy and it was as if someone just erased him from existence, it was that quick."

He paused and Jacob could hear him breathing fast on the other end of the line.

"Is this what you were trying to talk to me about before Jacob?"

"Yeah it was. Listen, have you heard of any more disappearances? Anything else weird?"

"I've been busy mate. There have been lots of disappearances. Just little articles in the paper coming at it from different angles but all essentially saying the same thing. I don't know why people aren't going nuts about this. I don't know why the media aren't screaming about this – do you reckon they've been gagged? Some sort of military thing going on and they've got their orders to keep quiet?"

"Maybe, I had thought of that but I think it's something worse than that. Barry, can you do me a favour?"

"Of course, my friend. I still owe you one for getting me out of that fight with the pub landlord all those years ago. But I always would anyway."

"Okay, your place has got just as much decent equipment as mine, but you're in the perfect place on the other side of the world. I need to know how this thing is working. Can you run a spectrum mineral test on the stratosphere." said Jacob.

"But what's that going to show? I'm sure they've said there was no difference in the lower level nuclei readings from..."

"It's not that I'm interested in" interrupted Jacob. "I think it's what's not there anymore we should be checking for. Look for gaps in the proton count, look for patterns in the count and if I'm right, God help us if I'm right, get back to me as soon as you can please mate okay?"

"No worries. Oh God, listen to me, there's that Australian influence coming in again, must really try and subdue that."

They ended the call and Jacob stared at Rebecca.

"We need to run a test at work. Like now"

Rebecca laughed, then stopped abruptly as she realised he wasn't joking.

"Er..Jacob? It's shut for the night, we can wait until tomorrow and then put a request in. It'll be fine."

"You said earlier the department was shut down and all personnel were allocated somewhere else. Do you think they're going to let me back into work after the way I behaved and start working on my own mad theory in a shut off department? And before you say it, you can't do it either. I've got a program already set up for this type of scan – you know I protect my own programs with the retina scan. It just needs tweaking a little bit to get it to do what I need it to do and then we're set. "

"This is madness. You're on the edge of getting sacked and now you want to break into the place?" She gawped at him as if it was the first time she'd ever seen him.

"Rebecca, this is important. Please. If I'm wrong, then you can call me an idiot, hand me over to security and have the pick of my stationery from my desk. But if I'm right and this scan shows what I think it shows...well then we're all in deep trouble and we all need to start looking elsewhere for answers on this thing."

Rebecca returned his gaze levelly. She had not seen him so serious about something for a long time. His brown eyes blazed with a fierce determination that she remembered from the days he first started in EFRS, in the days before Konrad started getting under his skin and undermining his every idea. She was liking this new Jacob and wondered about helping him out but the scientist in her was telling her to be cautious about jumping into this mad situation. Analyse it, the scientist voice said. Give it a couple of days, look at it from every angle, make sure you're right, *prove* that you're right before believing in this man.

"Rebecca", he said quietly, "trust me on this one. I need to compare results with what Barry's doing, that'll give us a global picture. We'll sneak in, get to the unit, I'll run the test, then we'll get right out of there. It'll take ten minutes tops. Please."

She bit her lip, and sighed deeply. "Come on then. But if you get me sacked, you can supplement my income for the next ten years."

CHAPTER NINE

It was midnight and they drove to the Research Station in silence. Both were dressed in black. Rebecca was still wondering how on earth she'd got into this ludicrous situation, especially as she was now dressed in Jacob's black Pink Floyd t-shirt turned inside out. The pink blouse she had been wearing wasn't the best outfit for breaking into buildings.

They rolled into a side street and killed the lights. Jacob was straight out the car and waiting for her by the corner before she knew it. She caught up and he nodded towards the canteen entrance. They had been through the plan earlier and she hoped that Jacob was right on this one otherwise this whole night was going to finish a lot earlier than they both expected. She loved her career and she couldn't believe she was putting it at risk by doing this stunt but she knew how much it meant to her friend.

Jacob crouched down by the bins facing the building as she crossed the road as silently as possible keeping to the shadows. The moon was a new one, weak and casting a pale yellow glow on the silent streets below. There was no sign of anyone in the streets, just a couple of cars in the car park. Jacob reasoned they must belong to security and late workers.

He saw Rebecca reach the wall nearest the canteen and pause, craning her neck round to see the entrance in the shadows. As he had hoped, the cleaner was outside having a cigarette. The lit cigarette glowed gently in the darkness. He had seen her a few times while on very long shifts last year and her routine was always the same, she must have got through 20 cigarettes in one night. He wasn't exactly sure how she got any cleaning done. She was sat on the wall ten feet away from the open canteen door, light spilling out from the kitchen inside. Her back was to the door, one hand held a cigarette limply while the other thumbed through pages on a mobile phone.

Rebecca took her chance and slid slowly round the wall and into the canteen. So far so good, he thought and waited for the signal.

It came less than two minutes later, a flash from her pencil torch indicating she was by the window. He ran across the grass to the outside of the building, keeping low. He heard a click, saw the pane of glass open and hoisted himself inside, glad for Rebecca's steadying hands when he nearly fell onto a desk of instruments.

"Thanks", he whispered and got his own pencil torch out. "I'm not as good as this spy stuff as I thought".

"Shut up and let's get this done", she hissed.

Jacob took the hint and they bent low keeping out of the sight of the windows towards their offices. She flashed her ID badge at the scanner and the door clicked open.

"God, how stupid am I? Now they'll know exactly who broke in, it'll be on the scan records." she whispered despairingly.

"Don't worry about that now, we'll just say you lost it somewhere and it was picked up" he replied as he uncovered his work laptop and went through security to open his list of programs, scanning his retina to gain access. The red glare of the scan flashed bright against the darkness of the room and they both winced.

"Okay, here it is, this is the one I need. I just need to set the parameters and get it running, should only take a couple of minutes."

"Fine, I'll check to see if anyone's coming", Rebecca said and darted off to the far end of the office by the door.

Jacob concentrated on the screen, a faint green glow illuminating his face as he studied the rolling figures in front of him. He entered another variable and held his breath. This is what it all came down to. He wiped away a bead of sweat rolling down his forehead but could feel his shirt sticking to his back.

The program finished its calculations and gave a soft beep. Jacob stared at the figures, sent a copy of it to his e-mail and exhaled slowly. He turned off the laptop and was just turning to tell Rebecca that he'd be ready in 30 seconds when the unthinkable happened.

His phone burst into life. Damn. It must be Barry.

He threw himself on the ground from his crouching position trying desperately to get his hand into his pocket to silence the ringing that sounded so deafening in the darkness. He was dimly aware of Rebecca running towards him, hissing at him urgently to shut up. He brought out his phone, only making the ringing louder and jabbed at the green display pleading for it to be quiet under his breath – *"shutupshutupshutup"*.

The phone stopped. The dark of the room returned for only a couple of seconds before being broken again by the beam of a torch light stabbing wildly through the blackness.

"Who's there?" the gruff voice shouted. "You shouldn't be in there."

"Dammit" cried out Jacob and he grabbed Rebecca's hand, "come on".

They raced down the corridor leading from the office away from the torchlight trying to keep fast but be as quiet as possible.

'Down here' she mouthed and pulled Jacob with her towards a small room containing old machines covered with bubble wrap. She prayed the door would be open and said a thankful prayer as the handle twisted in her grasp and they burst through.

Jacob glanced behind him to see the guard thirty feet behind coming in their direction. He was sure he hadn't seen them yet but it would only be a matter of time. He motioned for Rebecca to hide in the corner of the room near to the door but behind a large computer draped in sheets and more bubble wrap. She crouched down next to the fire extinguisher and he was just about to find a hiding place himself when the guard burst in, saw Jacob straight away and before he had a chance to move, slammed him against the wall.

Jacob saw Rebecca start to get up and flashed a warning look at her to stay down and keep hidden. It must have got across as she hunched below the computer desk again out of sight.

"I don't know what you think you're doing but you stay still mate. Who else are you with? How many of you are there?" the guard said leaning his full bulk onto his captive, pressing Jacobs nose into the wall so hard he was sure it was going to break.

"It's just me" Jacob managed to gasp, "get off me, you're hurting.."

"No bloody way mate, I'm calling this in. You shut up and stay still." He gripped both of Jacobs wrists together with one giant hand and reached for his radio.

Just at that point, Konrad walked in.

"I don't think there is any need for that, Sir. I can take cake care of it from here"

Jacob gaped at him, open mouthed. Again he saw Rebecca start to move from her hiding place but with an almost imperceptible nod, he motioned for her to stay down. He could see the confusion on her face – this was their boss. Why wouldn't they come clean? Surely they would be able to explain their way out of this with Konrad even if he did hate Jacob. And another thing, why wasn't Jacob coming clean to Konrad? He knew he should even though their working relationship was far from perfect but something stopped him. He thought of Konrad's sudden disappearance, of the results of the scan he'd just done that were clutched in his right hand. He decided to see how this played out.

The security guard bristled at the interference.

"Who are you then? Are you with these people?" he barked.

"These are my staff", said Konrad in a smooth calm voice, "they were obviously just getting in some late night work and you disturbed them. I'd prefer it if you didn't break my colleagues face on the wall if you don't mind"

The guard grunted and shifted his heavy frame backwards slightly, still keeping a firm grip on Jacob who was staring at Konrad, eyes narrowed.

"Show me your badge. If you work here, show me your badge" the guard said.

Konrad flashed his ID badge at him in the torchlight. As the guard relaxed his grip, Konrad noticed the piece of paper in Jacob's hands.

"What's that Jacob? What have you got?" he enquired smoothly.

"It's nothing. Let me go will you?" Jacob shouted and pushed back against the guard trying to get free.

"I thought you said they'd been working late, Sir? Have they been stealing things?"

"No, no it's fine…Raymond." Konrad was leaning forward and read the guards name badge in the dim light. "Can I have a quick word with you please?" He gestured to his office back down the corridor.

The guard's eyes darted suspiciously between the two men. He seemed to have lost control of the situation here and wasn't entirely sure what was going on. He knew something was wrong, there was something not right about this man's demeanour but he was willing to hear him out at least. The older man put a comforting arm around the guard and led him out of the door and into his office.

Rebecca could hear muffled voices and whispered to Jacob.

"What are you doing? It's our boss – let's just explain it's all a big mistake and he'll cover for us, I'm sure he will. Let me talk to him."

He shook his head firmly, clutching the scan results in his fist.

"I've asked so much of you so far Rebecca and I'm sorry to do that but please just let me deal with this. There's something not right here. There's just something not right. Stay down and keep hidden. Please."

She threw up her arms in an exaggerated pose but did was she asked. She had no idea why. This night was getting more confusing by the second and if she escaped all this with her job and sanity intact, she would consider herself lucky.

From the direction of Konrad's office there came a noise. They both whipped their heads round – it was unlike anything they'd heard before. It came twice. Short. Sharp. Like a furious bag of snakes that been kicked, Rebecca thought wildly. Then a thump that sounded like – well, like a body falling to the floor, she thought. She couldn't think what else it could be but...

Konrad appeared in the doorway smoothing down his white shirt. He flicked the light on and both Rebecca and Jacob narrowed their eyes against the sudden glare. Konrad Kaden did not. He stared levelly at his employee.

"What have you been doing here tonight Jacob? Why are you here?"

He glanced at the crumpled piece of paper in the younger scientists hands. Jacob said nothing. He was staring at Konrads eyes with fascination. He had always known the look in his boss's eyes before. There was usually a look of contempt there, sometimes boredom but they were always grey and flat. There was never any life there as if the many years of pushing paper around in the grey cubicle of his office had stamped out any spark of creativity and passion from his brain.

Now though, they were dancing. They were brilliant blue and sparkled in the vivid fluorescent as if – as if there were something truly alive behind them. He realised he wasn't breathing and let out a shaky breath.

"Where have you been Sir? Where were you yesterday?"

"I...I have been here. I was at work and I was here" he said matter of factly as if it was everyone else's stupidity that mean they couldn't see him.

"No, no you weren't Sir. The management looked all over for you, you weren't at work, you weren't at home. Where have you been? Can you remember?"

Konrad took a step forward. He was larger than Jacob by quite a way and his bulk was intimidating at the best of times. Now, with those dancing lights in his eyes, Jacob couldn't help but shiver despite the heat in the room. When Konrad next spoke, it was with a chilling tone in his voice that couldn't be mistaken.

"Jacob. You will give me that piece of paper. Now."

He held out his hand and continued to stare. Jacob noticed with a start that he couldn't remember the last time his boss had blinked. All sorts of alarm bells had started to ring in his head and he took a step back.

"I can't do that. I can't let you take it. Let me go past now. I need to leave".

Konrad advanced upon him, his arm still out ramrod straight. Something was rustling behind him as he walked but Jacob couldn't think about that now, he couldn't rip his gaze away from those eyes. He took another step backwards and felt his back hit the storeroom wall. He put the fist holding the paper behind his back and said "Let me get past. Now. You have to let me go."

Konrad's arm shot out to grab Jacobs arm in a vicelike grip. Jacob's arm burned and he lurched to the left kicking a leg out as he went. It connected with the other mans knee and he howled in pain. A chair was knocked over and Jacob used this to throw in front of Konrad as he approached again but the older man picked it up with one hand and threw it across the room.

Then that sound again. The mad vicious snakes. It filled the room, seemingly coming from everywhere until it felt to Jacob that it was inside his mind, it was all he had ever heard and he was going to be driven mad by it. Konrad – was it still Konrad? – drew closer. Jacob recoiled in horror as he saw the face in front of him changing, it was twisted by anger but it was more than that.

The eyes sunk deeper into the face. Large scales appeared on his – it's? – face and then disappeared under waves of rolling yellow skin. Jacob watched horrified, bile rising in his throat, as the eyes revolved backwards leaving dark protruding orbs that seemed to bore into his mind. The mouth was gone now too replaced by a gaping hole that was expanding. There were teeth inside still but small razor sharp one, row upon row. All of this happened in a couple of seconds but to Jacob, everything seemed to slow down. He realised two things simultaneously: firstly, he had been right all along. Secondly, he was going to die before he could warn anyone.

The mad snake sound reached a crescendo and Jacob shut his eyes, unable to move. Unable to breath. This was it.

The suddenly, the noise was gone, cut off instantly and the virtual grip on his brain was released. He felt the thing holding him slump to the ground at his feet and he opened his eyes to see Rebecca there, a fire extinguisher in both hands. The end of it was bloodied – was it blood? – with dark yellow thick liquid. As he watched, a large drip of the sludge hung from the end then dropped onto the still body of the thing beneath them with a heavy smack.

Rebecca looked at him for a moment, tears in her eyes, and Jacob knew she was fighting to keep her sanity. She sobbed once, looked down at the thing her boss had become and slammed the extinguisher down on its head again and again until Jacob shouted at her to stop. She looked up at him, eyes blazing. He stepped over the mashed body, took the extinguisher from her and held her. He could feel her quivering body against his as she cried uncontrollably. Just as their panic was dying down, there was a sharp hiss and the alien body behind them started to bubble and fizz. The thing that was Konrad melted into the ground until there was nothing left but the manager's clothes on the floor. Rebecca held her hand to her mouth and ran to the corner of the room, vomiting until there was nothing left to come out.

When Rebecca had calmed, he led her away from the body. He was sure it was dead – she had really made sure of that – but he wanted to get as far away from it as possible. Walking slowly to the door, they could now see the feet of the security guard protruding from Konrads office. One shoe was missing and the trouser leg rolled up where he had fallen. The skin itself was bone white as if made of china.

"Let's get out of here", Rebecca muttered and they made their way back to the car, lost in their own thoughts and too shocked to talk about what they seen. It was not until they were back at Jacobs flat, Rebecca had had a long hot shower and they were both nestling a vodka in their hands, that they began to talk about what had happened.

"Jacob, please tell me I just dreamed the last couple of hours. Tell me I'm safe in my bed and I didn't just bludgeon an alien thing with a fire extinguisher." She spoke with a tone of amusement to try and lighten the oppressive mood but her eyes were full of fear and confusion. "Did you know that was going to happen? Was that why you warned me to stay where I was?"

"God no", he said. "I knew there was something not right, especially after the scan results", he indicated the crumpled paper that neither of them had looked at yet, "but nothing like that.. that thing."

"So what did you find out? Why did he …it… want that scan result so much? What does it show?"

He rubbed his eyes with the heels of his hands. He would have to go to bed soon, it was now nearing 3am and his body ached all over but he didn't think there would be much chance of sleep tonight.

"I don't think it knew what it said. I just think it knew it was important enough for us to break in to the building at the dead of night and not want to hand it over. I'm not sure there was anything of Konrad left in that thing but it was smart. I could feel it trying to get into my brain, trying to get into my thoughts." He shuddered and folded his arms across himself, rocking back and forth gently on the edge of the bed.

CHAPTER TEN

Rebecca shivered and yawned. It had been a long night.

"I can't believe I've just met an alien", she said, "and, of course, killed an alien. Nope, never done that before. Come to think of it, I've never killed my boss before – two firsts in one night."

She thought about this rather startling fact for a moment.

"Jacob, what the hell is going on?"

"Let me call Barry first." Jacob stood up and walked slowly to the window, watching the raindrops make their way slowly down the pane. He dialled, had a short muttered conversation with his friend in Melbourne, shoulders sagging. He said his goodbyes, turned and leaned on the back of the chair facing his friend.

"Well, I'm more convinced now than I ever was but remember, I could still be wrong."

He paused. If he was going to say this without sounding mad – although after tonight, any theory was up for grabs in all probability - he wanted to get it right.

"Well, I got suspicious with the missing people. There's just too many at once. I'm amazed that people aren't noticing all these people going missing but then I figured that's just the kind of society we live in nowadays. Everyone's looking out for themselves and unless it's directly affecting them, people keep their head down and move on. It's only the famous people going missing that are getting people's attention but even then they're coming up with other excuses for what's going on."

He took a much needed drink, felt the cold liquid slide down his throat and continued.

"Then the missing people thing started to get even weirder. Michael Stipe went missing and it's his birthday. I looked up Mel Gibsons birthday – it was the day he went missing. The guy at the burger joint down town? He had a birthday badge on – I remembered it afterwards but it was definitely there."

"Unlike him", Rebecca muttered.

"Exactly. Okay. So far, so weird. That's when I started to connect it to the white light. What about if the light was just a distraction? It's certainly got everyone in the world talking about just one thing. The papers are still full of it, nearly one week on. It's all we're doing at work, everything else has been pulled. That's when I decided to do the scan. I figured if there was going to be something out there that we couldn't see – that we couldn't detect visually through displacement of stars or through heat signature – then maybe we could see something through an irradiated nuclei scan. That must show up something if brought up to maximum settings and pointed upwards rather than down into the earth where it is normally."

Rebecca looked confused. "And?"

"And it shows groups of nuclei travelling up and down to and from Earth. It goes up to somewhere a few miles above the surface. I could see two different streams of nuclei either way but that's only on this side of the hemisphere. Barry's just confirmed to me there's another stream on his side going up and another one coming down. The streams are miniscule but they're there. And here's the thing – they were travelling in groups of 232 per second."

"That rings a bell. Why does that ring a bell?"

"It did the same with me and I couldn't remember why for ages, then it hit me when I tied it in with the birthdays. 7 billion people on the planet right? 7.316 billion actually, it hit that a couple of weeks ago. I remember it being in the papers because that's the critical point at which population starts to multiply faster in the third world or something like that – some new study. Anyway, that figure divided by 365 is..." he got his phone out and went to the calculator app, "20,043,835. That's per day. Same number divided by 24 hours is 835,159. That gives you an hour. That divided by 60 to give you a minute is 13,919. And divided by 60 again to give you per second is..."

"232" said Rebecca.

"Well, 231.9888 actually but near as dammit."

Rebecca stood up and rubbed her temples trying hard to shake her tired brain cells into action. "So let me get this right? You reckon aliens are removing 232 people from the planet at a time because they read the newspapers?"

"Well, put like that it sounds stupid but it's just a weird coincidence. I don't know why it's that number, maybe it's their maximum upload speed, I don't know. Work that sum backwards though– if 232 people are removed every second – that's 232 out of 7 billion – it's a drop in the ocean. But over just one year, that's the entire population of the planet."

Rebecca frowned. "But you know that people would notice eventually?" she laughed. "It would get pretty empty round here by the end of the 12 months. "

Jacob smiled thinly. "Not if they were replacing the humans a couple of days later."

"Oh my God, of course. Konrad. The streams coming back down."

"Yep. I think we've proved beyond all reasonable doubt that he definitely wasn't human when he came back. It's such a good plan. Remove small amounts of people at a time; replace them before anyone gets seriously worried. Then, assuming the worst, when they outweigh the human population, they show their true colours and there's nothing we can do about it."

"And the birthday thing. That's how they're selecting the people. How on earth do they know that information?"

Jacob shrugged. "God knows. Maybe something genetic? But everyone in the public eye that I've checked out so far has gone on the anniversary of their birth. And it started with people on January 1st. How clinical. And it's been 4 days now. That's…" he consulted his phone again, "over 80 million aliens on the planet already. And 232 more every second."

Jacob looked out of the far window beyond Rebecca, watching the world outside illuminated by the street light. There were families out there who had lost a loved one, only for them to walk back in the next day. They would go back to normal, not knowing they had one of those creatures with them. A creature that is just waiting. Waiting for the right time to kill them. Husbands. Children. He looked back at Rebecca, who had gone pale.

"Jacob", she said, in a shaky voice, "it's my birthday in a weeks time."

CHAPTER ELEVEN

Twitter breaking news

March 13th

@reuters Michael Stipe welcomed back by ex band members of R.E.M. Singer says he "just needed some space to think"

@guardianuk Wife breaks down as film star Cuba Gooding Jr returns to family home. Cuba 'lost track of time'. Children 8 and 10 'over the moon and happy that Daddy is back'.

@bbcnews International Space Station astronaut clocks up 400 days in space. Cmmdr John Sudanski is fit and well but would welcome some excitement.

The second bright light came at 13.33 GMT and hit the globe the same as the first. This time it lasted seven seconds but that was enough to send the world into shock again. In Britain, there were riots in Manchester, in London, in Cardiff. The people were confused and demanded to know what was going on. In France, there was an impromptu demonstration outside the government offices in Paris. Across the globe, in China, the darkness was swept away and people fell from their beds, they ran screaming into the streets. The light came from everywhere all at once. There were no shadows.

CHAPTER TWELVE

March 14th

Chief Brady was having a bad day. He thought yesterday was bad when Konrad went missing and then he had to send Jacob home. This morning he had been told when he arrived for work that Konrads clothes were found in a storeroom by the cleaner. It looked as though he had been sleeping rough in there. On top of that, it looked as though one of the security guards had had a heart attack on duty. Police were looking into it but they were stretched tight at the moment. Unfortunately, that seemed to be life warming him up for today's heap of problems. The light came at lunchtime and his phone lines lit up like a Christmas tree.

The prime minister was on his private line within ten minutes. By the time the conversation had finished, Chief Alfred Brady was under no illusion that his job and the future of the department were not safe. They were not moving fast enough. The first light came a week ago and this second episode was driving people into a panic. Politicians don't like panic and an answer – any answer – would be expected from the research centre within 24 hours.

He sat at his desk staring at the telephone, sitting quietly on his desk. He had muted the ringer but could see the LED screen flashing as it obediently ignored whoever was trying to get hold of him now. He reached down, turned a key in his bottom drawer, opened it and took out a bottle of whiskey and a crystal glass that he saved for special occasions. He wasn't really sure this qualified but he needed something to take the edge off the day. He poured a generous amount and turned his chair to look out off his window across the city.

A couple of minutes later, he heard a commotion behind him and the door to his office opened with a bang. Damn, he had asked Susan to block all visitors and to divert all queries somewhere else. He turned and growled "I said I was not to be disturbed!"

Then he saw who was at his door and his day got a whole lot worse.

Jacob and Rebecca were there, resolutely fending off his receptionist and looking as though they hadn't slept in weeks. His anger rose, threatening to boil over and he felt the urge to throw his glass at his secretary. He managed to contain himself and glowered at her instead.

"I tried to stop them Sir", she explained meekly, "I told them you weren't seeing anyone."

Brady sat forward in his leather chair glaring at the two in front of him.

"That's okay Susan. Call security please. Tell them to come to my office. We have two ex-employees that need to be removed from the building."

Rebecca stepped forward. "Alfred, Sir. We need to talk..."

Brady stood up, knocking his glass over and off the side of the desk. It shattered on the black stone tiles making his secretary jump.

"It's Chief Brady to you, Miss Smith. It's 1.45 in the afternoon and you were supposed to be here at 8am. You were supposed to be helping the team." The last two words were spat out. "We have a situation. People are rioting. This all matters more than whatever you two are getting up to in your spare time."

"I beg to differ on that one Sir" said Jacob and Rebecca couldn't help but wonder at the tone of his voice – where had the timid man she had worked with had gone in the last couple of days. But then, this experience was changing them both so much, she barely knew who she was or what to think anymore. She knew she was scared though and that gave her resolve.

"I agree Sir." she said. "There are things that Jacob has to say – scientific theories – that you are going to want to listen to."

Brady bristled at this and barely kept his voice below a shout. "You don't come into my office and tell me what I should or shouldn't listen to. Mr Brooks, your work has been below par for many years now and I have no confidence that you can bring anything to this table that I need to listen to right now. Get out of this building and write me a report from home. I'll get someone to read it when they have time. And you, Miss Smith, I expected more from you."

"And I have more. Listen, we think we know what this white light signifies. And we know why people are disappearing" she cried.

"Disappearing people?" Brady exclaimed. "This is all to do with whatever he was blathering about yesterday isn't it?"

Alfred Brady had not managed to read a newspaper or listen to anything from the outside world for the last week. He had streams of information coming at him from all departments about the white light but he had been working at the research centre from 6am to 10pm every night, driving home and then crashing into bed. His wife kept telling him to slow down otherwise he would give himself a stroke but he was obsessed and the pressure from the journalists and politicians weren't helping at all.

"Listen", he said, sitting back down gingerly. He wasn't sure he was going to have a stroke but he knew he certainly had haemorrhoids. They always popped up to say hello in times of stress and they certainly weren't helping his mood.

"In deference to your hard work over the last few years Rebecca, I'm going to keep your job on hold but I want you to take time off now. Get your head straight, consult the union by all means if you feel you have to then come back and see human resources when you feel you can contribute in an meaningful fashion to what we are trying to do here".

"Sir, I'll be missing myself in a week. I may be back here but it certainly won't be me who's reporting back here, I think I would have been replaced by someone else."

"Absolutely right you would have been, I've got a waiting list as long as the Humber bridge of keen young scientists that want to work here." Brady was only half listening now; he had noticed his phone that had not stopped flashing since they started this ludicrous conversation – 18 missed calls – was now displaying 'Downing Street'. It flashed urgently at him for a few more seconds, then stopped. 19 missed calls.

Jacob spoke up now, his voice pleading with the older man. "Please Sir. Everyone's in danger here. You must listen to us; give me ten minutes of your time. Please."

Brady looked over Jacobs shoulder and saw his security team arrive with perfect timing. He raised his eyebrows and beckoned them in with one hand. The two guards walked in behind Jacob and seemed to fill the room with their presence. Their blue uniforms were pressed, their buttons shining and badges on their lapels showed them to be SFRS security. They were part of a daytime security detail that numbered fourteen officers. Ever since there had been false rumours of animal testing at the science centre, Brady had been forced to up the security and he had confidence that his team could see off any trouble.

The guards stood in front of the door to cut off any exit and watched Jacob and Rebecca carefully for any impending signs of violence. They weren't too worried. The man on the left that Brady had called Jacob was thin and wiry with brown hair that was currently all over the place. They recognised the lady from their rounds in the daytime – she often sat by the window and they both admired her looks from afar – and they were really secretly hoping to have some reason to grapple her to the ground.

Jacob held up his hands in front of his chest in surrender. "Look, there's no need for this. If you won't listen to us now, we'll e-mail you. I'll attach some scan results I've got. Please can you just do us a favour and consider what we have to say when you read it. It's to do with the light and concerns the whole population. And I'm sorry for disturbing you, Sir".

He had decided to back down in deference to the man's authority. He really didn't fancy being thrown out by the goons behind him either and he really didn't want them touching Rebecca. She was scared enough by her impending birthday without being roughed up by a couple of over zealous security guards.

They picked up the file they had brought with them which was lying untouched on Bradys desk and exited the room. The two guards stepped aside enough to let them pass and followed them out of the building to make sure they didn't cause any more trouble. Disappointingly for them, there was no more need for them and they returned to their security office to write the obligatory report on the situation.

Rebecca and Jacob returned to the car. They got in, put their seatbelts on and Jacob put the key in the ignition. Rather than turning the key, they sat there for a few minutes, each lost in their own little world. It was Rebecca that finally broke the silence.

"Jacob, we need to do something about this and we need to do it now. Without sounding like a bad science fiction movie, this planet is being taken over by ugly slimy aliens and I am not going to become one of them. I am just not. It's not a good look for a girl." Rebecca smiled and though the smile was genuine enough, he could see the worry and stress behind her eyes. This was taking a toll on both of them and he could see limited options on setting this right.

"Okay, let's go for the media. Brady was always going to be our best shot by a country mile and I can't believe he didn't listen to us but maybe the e-mail will help when I do that. The whole aggressive reaction he was giving us was probably my fault, I'm sorry."

"It's fine, Jacob", she said, holding his arm briefly and then letting her hand drop by her side. "Do you know anyone from the media? Anyone that will listen?"

"Well, that's the problem. I hardly read newspapers, never seem to have time for the things. And I certainly haven't met any media type people at parties."

Rebecca looked at him with a strange half amused look on her face which he caught out of the corner of her eye.

"What?" he said.

"Nothing." she said but she was openly grinning now.

He turned fully to look at her, the seatbelt biting into his shoulder.

"What??"

"It's just.." she attempted to make a serious face, not successfully, "I can't imagine you at a party. Do you even go to parties?"

Jacob made a mock hurt face. "I've been to parties."

"Many parties?"

"Many parties."

"You haven't, have you?"

"Okay, one party" he grinned, "but it was a damn good one. Dancing and girls and everything."

"And how old were you?"

"Ermm..seven. I'm very very good at the Birdy Dance, I'll have you know."

Rebecca threw her head back and laughed, something she thought she'd never be able to do in the circumstances. Again, Jacob was struck by her beauty. Her red hair tumbled down caressing her freckled shoulders and her eyes had joy in them for the first time since he could remember.

"Right, let's get this thing back on track then. We want to take this to the media to raise awareness of this mad situation, right?"

Jacob nodded.

"But what are we going to say? We're going to just ring up the Sun news line and say don't worry about the white light – you know that thing you devoted 40 pages to yesterday – and concentrate instead on the missing birthday people who are coming back as squidgy man eating aliens."

"They're not man eating."

"As far as we know. Oh, and by the way, those squidgy man eating aliens look exactly like the people that disappeared. So if you think your brother or your mum or your elderly nan is an alien you should kill them."

"Mmm, you could have a point. There is a small chance", he held his fingers a short distance apart to show how small, "that they may not take us seriously. What other options have we got? We've got to make people aware of this. If the authorities take this seriously, they can start looking into how to stop this. Or at least try and protect people."

"Who do we know that might know someone? My parents are non starters, they've been to less parties than you have – my mum's a librarian and my dad works from home as a web designer."

Jacob thought. "Well, my mum's dead so no go there and I haven't seen my dad for years. No brothers or sisters either. And not many friends" he added shamefully, "apart from Barry. We could try him, at least he believes us."

"Good plan", said Rebecca. "Give the nutter a call. What time is it over there? 11.30am? 12.30?"

"12.30 I think but he'll be up. He never seems to sleep."

CHAPTER THIRTEEN

A call to Barry was made and they were in luck. During his extensive social networking and excessive drinking when he was first in Melbourne, he had once struck up a conversation with a rather startled game show model called Stephanie at a party in a posh suburb he could no longer remember the name of. He had managed to ascertain, in his drunken state, that a game show model was a girl who pointed at prizes that you could win and demonstrated skiing equipment and the like to the contestants.

Stephanie the game show model had introduced Barry to Chris Fairbanks the host of her show, mainly to get rid of his Barry's advances. They had bonded over a love of red wine and now often kept in touch by e-mail, meeting up every few months to drink their way through a few bottles of burgundy and laugh at the absurdities of the media circus that now followed Fairbanks around.

While Barry was running his research lab, Chris Fairbanks had moved through the channels in his presenting career ending up with hosting his own talk show on ABC Australia on Saturday night primetime. It was successful for two reasons. The first was that Fairbanks was very good at his job, getting high profile guests to talk about their intimate secrets and forget they were on television. They never managed to forget they had a new book or film out though. The second reason was that "Fairbanks Talks to The Stars" was totally live.

Every Saturday evening, 30 million people sat down to watch Chris Fairbanks sit down with their favourite celebrities and interview them in a hilarious and yet sometimes surprisingly thoughtful way. It didn't hurt matters that he was very handsome, managing to combine that deadly combination of middle aged wisdom with a baby face making him much seem much younger than he actually was.

There was always the whiff of a scandal waiting around the corner with the show being live too. It had nearly being taken off air two years ago when Jordan Dean the pop star had sworn twice on primetime television. Only six months ago, Britney Spears walked off the set in a rage after Fairbanks had questioned her a little too robustly on her mental breakdown. There had been talk of applying a two minute delay in case of anything more scandalous happening but the head of the studio had refused this after seeing the latest viewing figures.

In short, Chris Fairbanks was the golden boy of Australian television, followed devoutly by half the population of Australia. And he was Barry's friend.

On Barry's request, they met in a bar called The Blue Egg, a dive in southern Melbourne they'd been going to for a few years now. The local clientele knew them there and mostly left Chris alone, although he would get the odd autograph request or teenager buzzing around, smartphone at the ready. More importantly, the barman knew them both and kept several bottles of red in the cellar for their visits. He prided himself on being able to surprise them with his choices and Chris and Barry enjoyed the opportunity to catch up with each other's news, relax and try out these new red wines in relative peace.

It was never that quiet in the Blue Egg, being the only bar in the area and especially not tonight. A rock band was cranking out tunes in the corner. The men hadn't caught the band's name but it didn't really matter, it was background noise to them although loud enough so they had to lean in to shout at each other for conversation. The lead singer said something unintelligible into the microphone and flicked back his long hair before launching into an unsteady version of Unskinny Bop by Poison.

Chris Fairbanks raised his glass of Uruguayan Red that had been provided to him and said "Cheers, Bazza." Barry returned the gesture with his glass – "Cheers Chris" and then together: "Down the hatch and pass 'em through the kill switch". This had been adopted about ten years ago after they were sat in a bar in similar circumstances and heard a rock band use this nonsensical phrase n one of their songs. They loved it and spent many hours trying to figure out what on earth it meant. They drank, considered the taste of the wine and made approving faces at each other and at the barman who was watching them from the other side of the room, an expectant look on his face.

They made small talk for a couple of rounds, just enjoying each others company without pressure of their respective jobs getting in the way. Their friendship was built on this and they rarely strayed into talking about work. Tonight, though, Chris was surprised when Barry asked him about what kind of guests he normally had on his programme nowadays.

"You still don't watch my stuff, Bazza? I'm hurt." And he pulled a hurt face just to show how wounded he really was.

"You know I'm too busy to ever catch your broadcast. And anyway, seeing you on television just freaks me out. No, I may have a guest for you if you're interested. Well, two guests actually."

"Hey, I don't get involved in booking the guests mate. I leave that to Mindy, she's the best in the business. You know who she got me last week? Daniel Craig and Sandra Bullock. Fantastic."

He leaned back in his chair, beaming at his friend and Barry caught a glimpse of the chat show host sparkle that he exuded on Saturday nights.

"Yeah yeah, I guess. But these people are friends of mine and they've got an interesting story. Probably the most interesting story ever."

Chris pulled a mocking amazed face and waved his glass in a circular motion to indicate for Barry to continue.

Barry was on insecure territory here. He wasn't sure how to pitch this to Chris, it sounded mad enough to him but then he had to the scientific background, the facts and the scan results.

"Okay. These two friends have solved the secret of the white light." He let this sink in for a few moments then continued. "And there's more. The white light is just a distraction. The real event people need to know about is the people going missing. They've worked out that people are vanishing into thin air on their birthdays – don't ask me why it's their birthdays, it just is.."

Chris nodded thoughtfully.

"and then being replaced...apparently... with aliens. Who look like the people they replaced."

"So that no-one knows any difference! Brilliant!" laughed Chris.

"Er...yeah", Barry continued uncertainly. "So anyway, they need to warn people and get scientists attention to stop this happening before everyone in the world..."

"become aliens", they finished together.

Chris grinned. "Bazza, that's brilliant. I've been saying to my producer all season we need a light hearted slot at the end of the show. I mean we've got the singing in the middle where I sing with a guest - did you see me do Me And My Shadow with Dame Judi Dench the other week? Doesn't matter – but this is great. This'll get people talking and talk is good". He became animated now, forgetting his wine and tapping something out on his phone.

"Where did you find these people?"

"Um.. they're friends of mine from back in England. I want to fly them over to talk to you, to talk to the media in general really."

"No way, mate. If they're coming over, I want them exclusively for me; I'm just texting Sandra now. If they can they get here for Saturday, I'll bump Jim Carrey to next week, he'll be fine".

Chris was in full flow now and although this wasn't going quite as Barry had hoped, at least they were going to get on the show and he guessed that was enough. Even if they were being paraded as a joke item to wrap things up, there was a chance that some of it would click into place for someone watching.

Chris looked up halfway through a text. "Hey, what was that about missing people? Missing people come back as aliens right?"

"Yeah, that's how they're doing it apparently. Nobody's noticed cos they're doing it in small numbers and then reappear. There's only a bit of a stir when famous people like Mel Gibson go missing."

Chris stared at him for so long that Barry thought he said something wrong.

"Mel went missing, you're right. I tried to call him that day and no one knew where he was. But he's back. And according to your friends, he's back because he's an alien!" He giggled in glee. "Bazza, you're a genius."

Barry smiled and went to the bar to order another bottle of red for them both. He texted Jacob while he was there and hoped they were all doing the right thing here. If Jacob was wrong – if they were all wrong – then they were going to look like prize idiots in 2 days time.

CHAPTER FOURTEEN

"Is there anything else you need?" said Captain Harris' wife, dropping him off at the airport that morning. He had another long haul today and they both dreaded it.

"No I'm fine thank you darling. As always, you're a lot better organised than I am. I'm sure one of these days I'll forget my uniform and turn up to pilot in my pyjamas." He grinned at his wife. "I'll see you in a couple of days anyway. This is the holiday I've been promising you for a very long time and I'm not going to let you down. This is going to be luxury, just you wait until you see the hotel we're booked in."

"I can't wait", she exclaimed, "I've been trying to find out about it ever since you told me about this holiday and I've got nothing out of you since"

She kissed him then. A long lovers kiss that belied their thirty years of marriage. He had joined the airline as a spotty twenty year old, straight out of flight school, worked his way up to co-pilot and for the last 7 years had been pilot of Virgin Atlantic 737 aeroplanes.

When he was a child, he used to lie in his back garden and watch the vapour trails of the aeroplanes above. His dad had bought him a special short wave radio that could pick up the chatter of the pilots miles above him and he spent countless days straining to understand the strange terminology used. Most of the chatter was confirming flight plans and altitude but occasionally there would be the thrill of light hearted banter between the cockpit and tower control and he would love these moments. At these times, he could almost see the pilots up there, coffee in their hands, joking with the pretty stewardess maybe. This was the life he wanted and he had pursued that dream relentlessly.

He looked his wife deep in the eyes and grinned.

"Do I kiss any better now I'm a 50 year old? They say that with age comes wisdom."

She ran a tongue over her lips and pretended to consider this.

"Mmm, not bad Jeff. But you've only been 50 for..", she checked her watch.. "about 10 hours. I think you might just be warming up. Maybe by the time I join you in that hotel in Melbourne, I'm hoping to get the full effect."

They embraced one last time and he retrieved his travel suitcase from the boot. He leant in to kiss her and then he was striding towards the terminal to check into the pilots lounge.

His wife watched him walk away, then turned the ignition to drive home and pack her own bags. It was to be the last time she ever saw her husband alive.

CHAPTER FIFTEEN

Jacob had been saving for years for a deposit on a house of his own. He had dreamed of one day being able to move into a nice house in the city. He imagined stroking the walls and knowing that they belonged to him. He would cut the grass and marvel at the lush green plants in his garden. More importantly, he would come home every night to spend the evenings with his beautiful wife. He was not ashamed that Rebecca had filled this role in many a daydream.

Now he was to support Rebecca in a different way. Barry had somehow managed to get them onto a talk show in Australia that apparently was huge news over there and Jacob had had no hesitation in transferring his savings into his current account straight away. He booked two tickets to Melbourne leaving early in the morning on Virgin flight 248. He hurriedly packed, not quite knowing what to take on an impromptu trip to Australia. Remembering the reason for his visit, he packed the only suit he owned and threw in a white shirt. He hoped that they had ironing boards in Australia.

Picking up Rebecca on the way, they arrived at the airport in plenty of time, eyes heavy with sleep but hoping to catch up on the plane.

When their time came to board and they stepped onto the shuttle bus to get to the aeroplane Jacob confessed he had never been on a plane before.

"Really?" Rebecca exclaimed, "I love planes. That's a Boeing 737, that's the new Dreamliner". She pointed at the aircraft parked around them. To Jacob, they seemed impossibly huge and he felt a shiver of fear run through him as he couldn't quite understand how such a gigantic thing could ever get off the ground.

"Well, you're a new discovery every day aren't you?" Jacob said as they walked up the steps into the aeroplane. They were greeted by a pretty stewardess who introduced herself as Caroline, checked their tickets and pointed left – standard class. He shrugged at Rebecca and then sidled between the other passengers putting their hand luggage away to make it to their allotted seats. At least it was a window seat. He admonished himself silently for being excited about being next to the window when they were on a flight halfway across the world to alert the world's media about aliens. A week ago, he was sitting in front of Eastenders with a pot noodle. Madness. He just hoped he wasn't outwardly managing to look like an excited child in front of Rebecca when she was so worried about the next few days.

"You're looking like an excited child", Rebecca said.

Jacob grimaced. "Sorry, I've just never been on a plane before."

He settled down and watched the steward run through the safety demonstration. He found himself giggling at the moment where he pointed out the exits here, here and here. Rebecca grinned at him.

He watched out of the window as the aeroplane started to move. The airport slowly rolled backwards out of sight as they taxied on to the runway. It paused there for a few minutes while they were waiting for the control tower to give them permission to take off and then they were off - the sheer power of the aircraft rolling down the runway and lifting into the sky. He loved the in flight magazine and the first couple of hours of looking out of the window. Seven hours into the flight, he had read the airline magazine twice, watched part of an American buddy cop film and watched Rebecca snore gently beside him for 10 minutes before his excitement finally wore off. Now he was just tired. Reclining his seat and plumping his travel pillow, he listened to the drone of the giant engines before finally drifting off to sleep.

In his dream, he found himself in front of a large door. An impossibly large door, made of wood with pock marks and dents in it as if it had once been the scene of a great battle, it towered above him. In fact, as he looked up to see the top of the door, he realised he couldn't see the top – it disappeared into the wispy clouds above his head. The sky was impossibly blue and hurt his eyes to look at it. He looked left and right. A wall stretched either side from the door as far as he could see. This was also impossibly tall but windows were cut into the walls at intervals and Jacob could see bright lights flashing from whatever was behind the door.

He looked for a bell or a knocker and could see nothing. He knocked on the door, a surprisingly loud booming noise that he could feel rather than hear – vibrations coursing through his body. Nobody answered but then he knew they wouldn't. He knew they were all having a good time without him inside. He pushed instead, a stupid idea for such a giant door but he was surprised when the door swung open easily. He stepped through.

Inside the giant door was a small room, confounding his senses. The walls were festooned with streamers and balloons as if it was a party. A beautiful chandelier hung from the high ceiling, its crystal droplets sparkling in the lights that were bouncing round the room. Jacob realised with a mind that seemed to be working at half speed that the crystal droplets were shaped like dolphins arcing out of the unseen sea.

The room was filled with people. He looked from face to face but couldn't recognise anyone he'd met before. They were dressed in suits and ties, was this what they called black tie? Jacob couldn't remember. Waiters pirouetted round the partygoers with trays of canapés and glasses of sparkling alcohol.

He suddenly noticed the music. Until now, the room had been quiet but now it seemed to burst into life. Balloons fell from the ceiling onto him and music and chatter filled his every sense. Couples whirled around him, smiling and laughing. He caught the eye of a lady in thick make up dancing on her own, her arms spiralling slowly round herself like Jacob had seen people in the park do of a Sunday morning. Was it taichi? He couldn't remember and it didn't seem important now. He was coming to realise that there was something important he had to do here. Or maybe it was someone important he had to meet.

He looked in front of him again and the crowd parted.

Rebecca was standing in front of him. She was impossibly beautiful. Her red hair was tumbling over her shoulders in ringlets and her blue eyes sparkled. She was wearing a black dress with hundreds of sequins in that caught the light and shone around the room. He noticed that everyone else in the room had stopped and was watching her. He didn't blame them. The music changed, softer now, and she held her hand out to him, beckoning him to her.

He stepped forward and took her hand. It was velvety soft to the touch. She looked him deep in the eyes and a connection was made, he had never felt so complete, so needed as at that moment on the dance floor. The music slid into a Viennese waltz and without thinking, Jacob slid a hand round Rebecca's waist and they started to dance. Her body was close to him and his head was swimming with her perfume, his every sense alive with the knowledge that they were together and it felt real. It felt perfect. The other couples on the dance floor joined in now whirling and spinning like teacups in a fairground ride, their faces blurring as Jacob and Rebecca span round, their eyes still locked into one anothers.

The music eventually stopped and the other couples fell away into the background talking quietly to themselves in deference to the couple left standing on the dance floor. The corners of Rebecca's mouth turned up slightly in a smile and Jacob knew she was going to kiss him. Her gaze flickered to his lips and then back to his eyes and she leaned in parting her soft lips.

He closed his eyes.

As he began to kiss her, the perfect kiss, he became aware of a noise. An irritating noise. He tried to concentrate on the perfect kiss but the noise was getting louder and it wasn't supposed to be there. It was an angular noise, sharp with jagged edges. It hurt his ears and clashed with the soft classical music in the room. He tried to focus his mind on the kiss but the sound was everywhere now, hissing in his brain, and seeping into his pores.

He opened his eyes to see Rebecca, his love, smile at him again. But the sparkle in her eyes was gone. Instead, lights were there, dancing, behind her pupils. Her beautiful pale face morphed into a wave of foul smelling rotten skin, her eyes rolling back to reveal dark orbs that seemed to spit fury at him. Her mouth, that he had been kissing only moments before, expanded rapidly to reveal rows of razor sharp teeth and he could see a thin black tongue flicker inside. She – *it?* – leaned in to kiss him once more, to devour him. As he found himself frozen in horror, her gaping mouth latched onto his throat, her hands clung onto the top of his head and he could feel claws begin to dig into his skull – almost moulding them into him. His blood was being sucked out of him, his life force was going and all he could think of was Rebecca.

"Rebecca!" he shouted and sat up with a start, sweat pouring from him. He looked round wildly to see the other airplane passengers staring at him alarmed. He felt a hand on his arm. He span his head round to see Rebecca, looking at him in a concerned fashion.

"Are you okay? Jacob?" she said, shaking his arm gently as he slowly regained his senses.

"God, I'm sorry, I'm...woah, I just had the weirdest dream".

"More like a nightmare by the sound of it."

"Was I...did I say anything?" he asked, thinking of the way she looked in his dream when she held her hand out to him.

"You were muttering a few things. I couldn't really catch the words really" she said, but the way she blushed and looked away told him she wasn't telling him the whole truth.

He exhaled and wiped his forehead with a napkin. A stewardess appeared at his side without being summoned, crouched down on her haunches and enquired if he was okay. He ordered a glass of whisky and tried to forget his nightmare.

CHAPTER SIXTEEN

Twenty one hours into the flight, Captain Harris stretched his arms to the cockpit roof and yawned loudly.

"Do you have to do that so dramatically, Jeff?" said his co-pilot.

"You know it's one of the many things you love about me Ben" grinned Jeff. "I can't help it. I always start dying slowly of boredom this many hours into the flight. The autopilot's on, the passengers are snoring and all we've got to do is check the wings are still on occasionally."

"Are the wings on, Captain?"

Jeff twisted sideways to look out the window to his right.

"Wings are on, Co-Pilot Ben".

"Brilliant. That's one less thing to worry about then. You must be looking forward to your holiday."

"I am indeed. That beach is calling to me."

"I can't believe you haven't been to a beach for years. I couldn't go that long, I need my piece of sun every 4 months or so otherwise I get twitchy. And a twitchy pilot is not a good pilot."

"Yeah, I know. I'm hoping this will be the holiday of a lifetime – I feel like I've spent a lifetime worth of wages on it. I sometimes feel like I'm married to this job more than I'm married to my wife, which incidentally is a point she's made to me many times over the years, and I so need this holiday."

"When was the last holiday you had then? Surely it can't have been that long ago."

Jeff raised his eyebrows. "You reckon? We've been married for thirty years now and we last went on holiday together on our honeymoon."

Ben stared at him. "You're kidding" he said.

"Nope. 1983. We got married on the Saturday, slept over in the hotel – well, mostly slept – and then on the Sunday morning we made it to our hotel. Guess where?"

Ben shrugged. "No idea. Spain? France?"

"Milton Keynes."

Ben put down his coffee carefully on the floor of the cockpit and leant forward resting his folded arms on his knees.

"You have got to be kidding me. What in hells name possessed you to take your new wife there?"

Jeff grinned. "My brother owned it. We had two nights in the Blue Bay hotel in Milton Keynes, free food and drink and he even reserved exclusive use of the pool table for us. To us right then, it was heaven." His eyes turned misty as he thought back. "Okay, you think about it now and you're right, it was ludicrous but that's what love does to you mate. We were so wrapped up in each other, you could have put us in a glue factory and we wouldn't have noticed."

Ben smiled and reached into his jacket pocket.

"Enough sloppy stuff, you old man. Here, I nearly forgot. Happy birthday Jeff." He handed over a card and small package in brightly coloured paper.

"Ah, you shouldn't have", Jeff said in a tone of voice that made it quite clear he certainly should have.

He slid a finger across the top of the envelope and pulled out a pink card with teddy bears on. He looked at Ben quizzically.

"Sorry, Chelsea chose it." he said, referring to his 6 year old daughter, Jeff's god-daughter.

"It's lovely."

He turned the small package over, locating the taped down flaps. He opened the first flap, looking at his co-pilot expectantly....and then promptly vanished.

The small present dropped to the floor in the cockpit followed by a pair of headphones and microphone. The large dent in Jeff's leather chair slowly re-inflated.

CHAPTER SEVENTEEN

Rebecca stretched, her joints cracking. Nearly a day in an aeroplane seat took a toll on your body and she just wanted to get out into the Australian sunshine and walk around. Try as she might, she couldn't get the thought of her birthday out of her mind. 4 days, 93 hours away. If it was going to happen, would it happen on the stroke of midnight? Would it hurt? And if she materialised up in space, would she come face to face with another one of those hideous alien things. She couldn't actually believe she was thinking of these things as if they were real. The logical side of her brain scoffed at her every time she tried to think deeply of the situation she was in. After the night at the research centre, however, she knew it was real.

She glanced over at Jacob who was watching some comedy film on the screen in front of him. His headphones were on and he was staring intently at the television but he didn't look as though he was really concentrating fully on it. She wondered what was going through his mind, she knew he was worried about whether everything he had said was correct and he was definitely worried about her.

She remembered the first time she had met him at the Research Centre. She had been working there herself for eighteen months with another lady called Sue. She had got pregnant, decided not to come back and the new guy was drafted in to replace her.

Rebecca was irritated at first with the replacement – this thin wiry haired young lad who blushed every time she spoke to him. It had taken a few days before he had even managed to speak to her – coming across to ask her if she knew how to work the spectrum analyzer. She remembered being confused. With the experiment they were working on and the brief they had been given, there was no need to go near that apparatus. She asked him to explain why he needed it and with his cheeks burning red, he explained his theory. It flipped the experiment on its head and that day, she saw a glimmer of his brilliance. Konrad Kaden noticed that day too and he started treating Jacob with suspicion at the same time that Rebecca started to treat him with respect.

It had taken several months for him to speak to her whilst looking her in her eyes. Gradually they became firm friends and now spent more and more time together, catching regular meals in fast food restaurants at the end of the working day so that they could relax and gossip about their colleagues. She knew he wanted more than friendship from her but while they were still working together, she would never allow it; that had always been her number one rule. Also, it was kind of nice having him follow her round like a little lost puppy sometimes. It did a girl's self confidence wonders.

Looking around the plane now, taking in the slumbering passengers and the wispy clouds out of the far windows, she noticed two stewardesses having a conversation. They were obviously disagreeing about something and one of them had a clipboard with her and running her finger down some kind of list. Then she pointed to the clock on the front wall – Rebecca followed her gaze – which said 7.21am. Realisation seemed to dawn on the other woman's face. She looked alarmed and disappeared back behind the curtain that separated standard class from first class. The other lady, summoned by a service light a couple of rows in front of Rebecca, walked down the aisle and resumed her duties, taking a drinks order from a bald headed gentleman.

Rebecca pushed her service light and when the stewardess came to her, she enquired if everything was okay.

"Sorry, Madam?" the stewardess said.

"I just wondered. You looked a little concerned up there that's all. Just checking everything was okay on the plane that's all."

"Oh yes, madam. Everything's fine, we should be landing soon. Would you like a drink?"

"No thank you, I'm fine", Rebecca said. She wasn't entirely convinced by the stewardess but the plane still seemed to be flying smoothly so it couldn't be all bad. She returned to reading the in flight magazine for the third time.

It was about ten minutes later that she heard the first scream coming from the first class section. People in their section sat up, woken from their stupor and stared at the curtain dividing the aircraft. Rebecca suddenly noticed that there were no cabin crew around and she shook Jacob by the arm. He started, took off his headphones and looked at her troubled expression.

"What's wrong?" he said.

Before she could reply, the curtain was drawn back in front of their section and a stewardess with a drawn face stepped through. She was flanked by what looked like a senior cabin manager and another stewardess that looked as though she had been crying.

"Can I have your attention please ladies and gentlemen? Everyone's attention please. Due to a medical incident in the cockpit, I have to ask the unusual question – is there anyone on the plane who has had experience in flying an aeroplane?"

The passengers gasped and again a lady a few rows back from Rebecca gave out a short scream. There was a loud muttering amongst the people in the section and a man in the front row started to urgently argue with the senior cabin manager. Jacob wasn't sure what could come of arguing with the staff but he guessed it was stress. So there was no-one flying the plane? Where was the co-pilot for goodness sake? A chill ran through him and he could feel the hairs on his arms stand up as he suddenly visualised the aeroplane flying through the air without anyone in control, thousands of feet above the earth. He was vaguely aware of a man sobbing quietly to his right.

He looked over at Rebecca to see how she was feeling. To his surprise, she was shakily raising her hand. Her face had gone pale, and he could see beads of perspiration on her temple.

"What are you doing?", he hissed. "You can't fly. Can you?"

She had her hand up fully now and people were starting to turn and look at her.

"It was my dad." she whispered to him. "He always wanted to fly. Never could because of his bad eyes so he paid for me to have flying lessons instead. But that was years ago."

"Please tell me you had more than one lesson"

She rolled her eyes at him. "I had more than one lesson".

The stewardess reached her and crouched down beside Jacob looking past him to speak to Rebecca.

"You know how to fly Madam?"

"It's been a while but, yes, I had lessons and I know my way round a cockpit. Well, a light aircraft anyway."

"Please can you come with me", she said and stood up. Rebecca also stood up, wincing from using her legs for the first time in many hours. A smattering of applause rang out and an elderly lady behind her leaned forward and squeezed the hand that was on her headrest causing Rebecca to blush a deep red.

"I need my friend to come with me please", she said to the stewardess.

"I'm afraid non cabin crew aren't allowed in the cockpit."

They both looked at her and Rebecca raised her eyebrows.

"Of course, sorry, you're right" said the stewardess apologetically. "Would you both like to come with me please?"

They made their way up the aisle and into the first class section where the passengers again applauded them. Now they had the grace to both be embarrassed and Jacob even leant across to one middle aged man to mutter "It's not me. I don't know how to fly."

They passed through another curtain and into the cabin staff quarters where a thin steward who was visibly shaking leant over and clasped Jacob in a damp handshake.

"Thank you", he said.

"It's not me!" Jacob said, exasperated.

The head steward glared at the other member of staff and they reached the cockpit door. A key code was entered and the three of them passed into the cockpit. They had to duck under the low doorway and also step over a small step, a feat that managed to baffle Jacob as he hit his head gently on the metal surround.

Jacob and Rebecca gasped at the scene in front of them. A wide array of buttons and dials greeted them and out of the large windows, they could see white clouds and brilliant blue sky. Jacob had to grab onto the wall - from the cockpit, you could really tell how high up you were, there was no escaping it.

A man was crouching on the floor taking the pulse of another man in pilots uniform slumped in the corner. A bandage was wrapped around the injured man's head and it was clear that he was out cold.

"What happened? Is that the pilot?" enquired Rebecca.

"Hang on a sec", said the head steward and he reached past her to close the door and lock them in. With 5 people in the cockpit, it was now very crowded and Rebecca had to hold onto a metal case on the wall to keep herself upright as the plane rocked slowly. She noticed a smear of blood next to where her hand was and drew back.

The steward turned back to them.

"Okay guys, I'm really hoping you can help here. My names Tim by the way." He was tall and thin with dull brown eyes. In his late thirties, he had been at the airline for over ten years and still loved every minute of it. He had survived a couple of minor scares before where engines had failed but nothing like this. This was the stuff of nightmares. He was proud of his staff though, they were a close knit crew, and he was sure that they were keeping the passengers calm in the seating area. Right now, keeping everyone calm was essential.

Rebecca and Jacob introduced themselves and Tim continued.

"Okay, well, the long and short of it is that we don't quite know what happened. Jane here –" he indicated the stewardess who had brought them into the cockpit – "noticed the flight time was off, as in we should be preparing for landing by now. She brought the matter to my attention and we came to see the pilot to check if we'd had to alter course for any reason. It happens sometimes and it's our job to let passengers know the reason for the delay"

He ran a hand through his hair and continued.

"Anyway, when we reached the cockpit, there was no reply on the intercom. And looking through here – "he indicated a tiny peephole in the door – "we couldn't see anything. That was when alarm bells began to ring."

Giant bells had been ringing in Jacob's mind for a while now and he thought he could see where this was going. He hoped against hope that he was wrong though.

"When we got into the cockpit, there was no sign of Captain Harris and Co-pilot Stelling here was out cold on the floor. It looks as though he hit his head on this controller cabinet here but I can't understand how you can knock yourself out on it. I mean, it's hard metal and everything but it's right behind him, He must have been almost running into it."

"And where the hell is Captain Harris?" said the steward on the floor tending to the co-pilot. "How can he just vanish from a locked cockpit on an aeroplane? It's not like he got bored and parachuted off, is it? My God, what a mess." He was visibly shaking and was trying unsuccessfully to keep the panic out of his voice.

"So that's why we need you, Rebecca. What flight experience have you had?" Tim asked.

"I'm sorry", Jacob cut in, "but you lot come up in planes every day. Surely you must have some idea how to fly this thing. And isn't there an autopilot button that lands you? I'm sure I've heard of that."

Tim smiled wanly.

"Well, good questions. Captain Harris likes to do the taking off and landing himself, especially on long haul flights – otherwise they're both just sat here and monitoring dials for 23 hours. The autopilot is still on which is why we haven't plunged to the ground yet but when we disengage it, we can't set the autoland without the Captains code."

"And you can't land a plane?"

"There's supposed to be courses being set up next year for two staff per aircraft to have the necessary training. We've asked around the crew and the best we came up with was 2 goes on the flight simulator at the start of training. That's why we need you." He said, turning to Rebecca again with a hopeful expression on his face.

Rebecca exhaled. She was feeling dizzy and this whole situation didn't feel real but then since when was that a problem over the last few days.

"Well, as I was saying to my friend here, my Dad always wanted to learn to fly. He was obsessed with planes but he failed the eye test to join the RAF when he was a teenager. Or at least to be a pilot anyway. He mucked around in the radio corp with them for a few years but always looked on enviously at those people taking off from the airfield everyday. Anyway, as soon as I was old enough, he paid for lessons for me. I qualified in a Cessna 150, flew about 200 hours I guess."

Tim nodded and looked relieved.

"But that was 10 years ago," Rebecca hastily added. "And I've no idea how to fly this thing. I mean, I guess the general theory is the same. But, oh God, all these people aboard. And the size of the thing."

"Don't worry" the steward crouching on the floor said "you'll do a better job that anyone else on this plane I'm sure. If I can get Ben here to regain consciousness, we'll see if we can get some sense out of him to help."

"We've radioed down to control. They're aware of the situation and have got a retired pilot on the ground ready to help you out. They're confused as us regarding the whereabouts of Captain Harris but we're just going to have to deal with that when we get down."

He indicated towards the pilots seat and looked at Rebecca. She felt like she was going to faint. Shakily, on legs that felt like rubber, she took her place.

Despite her terror, the view was spectacular. From this high up, she could see the curvature of the Earth so clearly. Small wispy white clouds were scattered beneath her and the sun was coming over the horizon away to her east. Below the clouds, she could see green land to her right and the blue sea sparkling at her from below as if someone had scattered a million diamonds in it.

The view in the cockpit was less welcoming. There were buttons and dials everywhere, she had never seen so many. Lights were blinking at her and computer readouts were giving her all sorts of information she may or may not need. To her left was a large handle she knew was the throttle but even thinking about touching that terrified her. To her right was a highly detailed map stuck onto the leather surround of the window showing their route. This was duplicated by a moving map in front of her showing the same thing. A vast array of knobs and switches peeled away to her left and when she looked up at the roof, there were more, steadily blinking at her. All waiting for her instructions.

Despite her previous experience, she couldn't imagine even flicking one switch here. One wrong move and it may send them all plummeting to their deaths. The one that terrified her most was the steady red light down by her knees. 'Autopilot On' it said. There was no way she could imagine touching that one.

"Okay, we need to give this lady room. Jacob, if you'd like to sit in the other chair but please don't touch anything unless you know what you're doing as well." Ted said. Jacob's terrified stare answered that one for him. "Jim and Susan, can you take Ben out into the staff quarters? Thanks".

He sat down on the floor between the two seats in a yoga position. To Jacob and Rebecca's mind, this was all getting more surreal by the minute.

"Okay Rebecca. As I said, we've contacted the tower and they've got an ex-pilot standing by. If you put on the headphones and press that button by the mike socket, that gets you through to them. I know that much. God speed."

Rebecca looked across at Jacob, smiled worriedly and put the head phones on. She pushed the grey button next to the microphone socket and jumped as a voice filled her ears.

"Virgin flight 248, Virgin flight 248, are you receiving me?" said a man's voice. It was slow and drawled, reminding Rebecca of John Wayne.

The accent shocked her so much, she blurted out :"Why are you American?" before she could stop herself.

"Well, it's nice to know you're focusing on the big things up there. You're right, I am American but live out here in Australia now. Can I just confirm I'm talking to Virgin flight 248 please? For the record?" He pronounced I'm as 'ah'm' and something in his voice relaxed her already.

"Er..yes sorry. This is Virgin flight 248. My names Rebecca. Rebecca Smith."

"Well hello Miss Smith. I'll call you Rebecca from now on if you don't mind. I may need to give you some instructions fast and I don't want to slow things down calling you Miss Smith all the time, do I? My names Maximillian but I certainly don't want you calling me that either. Max is fine. Are we good?"

"We're good."

"Okay Rebecca. One of the flight crew up there has already told me what you've done in the past and this ain't going to be much different, just a few more buttons here and there. Now Rebecca, listen to me. Are you listening?"

"I'm listening"

"Okay. Throughout everything I'm about to tell you, I want you to remember one thing. You can do this – you will land this plane. Okay? Sound good to you?"

"Yeah. I can land this plane." She said and surprised herself by sounding more confident than she felt. She indicated to Jacob to put his headphones on too so that he could listen in.

"Well Rebecca. I can see you on my screen here. You've overshot Melbourne airport by 120 miles so we're going to try for Onaluwa airport instead, it's about 10 miles away to the east. You've got plenty of fuel so that's one less thing to worry about."

"Good. "

"Good indeed, Rebecca. Now, can you tell me your altitude please? It'll be on the dial directly in front of you, just south of your normal eye line."

"It says 21500 feet." Just saying that out loud brought on a fresh wave of dizziness and she closed her eyes briefly to regain her sense of calm.

"That's good Rebecca, just great. I can see the same figures on my screen here and I've got a picture up of your exact instrument panel so it's just like I'm up there with you okay?"

"I like the sound of that." she said.

"Now run me through the other readings you can see."

As Rebecca confirmed the other readings around the cabin, Jacob sent a little prayer up to a God he had never believed in. He hoped He would forgive him. After all, if they ever got through this, they would be doing humankind a big favour. Or at least, that was the plan.

"Now Rebecca", came that American drawl again, "here's the fun part. Please can you push the button that says autopilot and enter the code 7841. That gives you manual control. You'll hear a click from the button, a beep then the plane will dip slightly. Not enough so much as the passengers will feel it, but I'm sure you'll feel it from where you're sitting. If you 'd like to do that for me now please Rebecca." His voice was clear and calm, just what Rebecca needed. She summoned up all her courage and pushed the button.

CHAPTER EIGHTEEN

Four hundred miles away, Barry was taking a quick lunch break – couscous and a handful of berries never took that long to consume – when he noticed a picture on the television screen in the corner of his staff room.

It was a stock photo of an aeroplane and below it were the words "Aeroplane Emergency. Flight 248 being piloted by passenger – live updates". There was something familiar about that number and he flicked on his phone to check his past messages. His stomach lurched as he re-read the one from Jacob the day before. It was their flight.

He picked up his keys, told his secretary he was leaving for the day and ran to his car.

***

The aeroplane dipped, just as Max had said it would, but Rebecca still gave out a little scream under her breath. She gripped onto the circular steering wheel in front of her – the yoke she reminded herself – and held it tight, knuckles white. The engine noise changed too. The constant reassuring rumble lowered in pitch and the cockpit rattled briefly before settling into its new rhythm.

"Good girl Rebecca. I hope you've got hold of the yoke there because I'm going to ask you to gently turn the plane in a minute. Not too much, we don't need aerobatics from you today. Just nice and steady. Have another look at the heading dial in front of you. I need you to turn the plane east so that the heading reads 225. Are we cool with that?"

We are so not cool with anything, thought Rebecca but she answered him in the positive anyway. She gradually began to turn right –east – and kept an eye on the heading dial just like he said. 215 – 217 – 222. She turned the yoke back again slowly until it settled on 225.

"New heading 225, Max" she said, letting her inner mind cheer and whoop with this small victory. Out of the corner of her eye, she could see Jacob give her the thumbs up. Maybe they could do this. If all she had to do was follow these simple instructions, then maybe they could do this.

That was when she saw the flock of birds.

"Oh God Oh God Oh God" she chanted.

"What is it? Rebecca?" Max said, his calm disappearing a little now as he recognised the panic in her voice. "What can you see?"

"Flock of birds." She managed to say. "Huge flock. Coming straight for us."

"Birds. Goddammit." She heard him muttering and then "Okay Rebecca, you need to manoeuvre out of their way and quick. If they're above you, go down. If they're below, go up. Quickly but not drastically."

They were coming at her fast from slightly below her but still in the aeroplanes path. She knew that if even one bird got in the engine, it could blow the engine out. One fan in there breaks off and sends pieces flying into the other fans then all of a sudden you're flying with one engine on fire.

She pulled back on the yoke and the engine whined at her. The nose rose up sharply, too sharply, and a red light came on to her right. She grimaced and brought the nose down again slightly checking the altitude as she did. 300 feet higher, she hoped that was enough.

She couldn't see the birds anymore but they must be almost on her now. She looked back at Tim, her teeth clenched together and eyes scrunched up with tension.

Tim had just started to say "Do you think we missed.." when the first bird hit and Rebecca cried out. The bird – she thought it was a goose – hit the nose cone and bounced high over the plane followed by three more flying just over the cockpit. Another couple hit the bottom of the plane right under where they were sitting. The sound was huge in the cockpit as if a giant was banging on the underside demanding to come in. And then....nothing. Jacob scrambled up out of his seat and peered out of his window to look back at the engine.

"All looks good this side. No alarms going off either." He said.

Rebecca was sat staring straight ahead, eyes wide open. She was breathing very slowly and deliberately through her nose to stop from fainting. They didn't need another prone body on the floor.

"Tim", she asked in a quiet voice. "Please can I have a cold water?"

Tim passed her the water and she drank it all down, slowly, letting the cool liquid wake her senses and calm her down. At one point, she thought her stomach was going to rebel and bring it all back up again but it settled.

"How ya doin up there Rebecca?" said Max in her earphones. "Still with me?"

"Yeah, I'm still here Max. Let's get this thing on the ground."

"That's m'girl."

***

Barry had the news on his radio blaring out at him as he sped down the motorway away from Melbourne. He had called in a favour at the airline, found out where the plane was heading and was now listening to news reports as he travelled there. They had nothing new to report at the moment but he wanted to keep up to date just in case.

***

Rebecca finished the last of the instructions Max had set her and grinned across at Jacob.

"Hey, that's great Rebecca" Max said. "We're now on course for the airstrip and at the right speed. We'll be there in about ten minutes and I need to run through a few bits and pieces along the way"

"I'm listening."

"Good. Now I can see you on my monitor here and I'm in the tower so soon I'll be able to see you coming towards me."

Rebecca raised her eyebrows in surprise. She had assumed Max was back in Melbourne but was glad. If they got through this, she was going to give him the biggest hug he'd ever had.

"When it gets to the right time" he continued "I'm going to ask you to gently reduce the power and reduce altitude. We'll continue that until you're coming in nicely to the strip. And Jacob?"

Jacob perked up at the sound of his name. He didn't realise Max even knew he was there but I guess Tim had told him at the same time as filling in about Rebecca's flight experience.

"Yes?"

"Jacob, I know you've never done this before but I'll have a couple of jobs for you. Nice easy ones but I need you to get them right okay? No sitting around and watching your friend do all the hard work".

He could hear Max chuckle softly in his ears.

"Yep, that's fine. I'm all good" Jacob replied, although he was anything but.

The three of them ran through the landing routine several times before Max spoke out again.

"I can see you. You're coming in beautifully Rebecca"

They both peered through the cockpit and saw the airport in front of them dead ahead, small on the horizon but coming in fast. Rebecca was more worried about the buildings to the left and right of the airstrip. She called back to Tim.

"Any sign of life from that co-pilot Tim? I could really do with him waking up about now."

Tim went to check.

"Sorry, still out cold. We need to get him to a doctor when we land." He said.

'When we land' thought Rebecca. I like his optimism. Well, they were definitely coming down one way or another.

"Right, here we go Rebecca. We've practised the landing procedure, just think of the plane as that old Cessna you used to fly okay? Now, ease back on the throttle a bit. Let's get you down safe, shall we?"

Rebecca reached out with her left hand and gripped the large throttle handle. She pulled back gradually and heard the engine noise lower in pitch. Max kept the positive spin in her head and she was very appreciative of this. Right now, she couldn't feel her arms and the muscles in her neck were screaming at her from being so taught with stress. She brought the plane down to 5000 feet and made sure she was lined up with the airstrip.

"Hey, I think we might have a welcoming committee, Rebecca", Jacob said.

Either side of the airstrip, at a respectful distance, were fire engines, ambulances and a myriad of other emergency workers in bright neon jackets. Max told her that it was standard procedure to call out the emergency services for an incident like this but it didn't mean that she should fear the worst. They were still a couple of miles away but could see the throng of people waiting for them.

"I'm not sure whether that makes me feel better or worse" Rebecca groaned.

Max piped up then.

"Rebecca, you're at the perfect height and speed there. Let's get the wheels down shall we? It's time to land this baby. It's the button to the right of the flaps, red and circular."

"Okay, I've got it." She said and pushed the button. An angry scraping sound came from the underside of the plane filling the cockpit. Jacob looked round in alarm and Tim stood up. A red light started flashing above their heads and an alarm sounded mixing with the scraping noise. "What the hell is that?" she screamed.

"Rebecca?" Max was saying above the din. "Rebecca, I need you to push that button again, my darling." His voice was still so calm. She did as she was told and the deafening noise stopped abruptly.

"Now don't panic on me but I think your landing wheels are stuck." He said.

"Those bloody birds", Rebecca muttered and put her head in her hands.

Jacob couldn't believe this. He looked at the ground longingly, he would do anything to be down there right now, kissing the earth.

"Rebecca, I need you to do another turn while we sort this out." Max said.

"No." She said surprising herself. "I'm coming down now. I want out of this. Talk me down Max"

Max thought about arguing with her but the tone in her voice convinced him how close she was to breaking point. Better to have someone up there who wants to get down rather than someone who has given up and not thinking straight.

"Rebecca, you need to do exactly as I say. You're half a mile from the airstrip, I need you down to 1000 feet right now, steady as she goes and get that airspeed down, you're coming in fast. You'll see some activity on the ground, don't worry about that."

She certainly could. Trucks were now hurriedly moving up the landing strip pumping out thick foam everywhere. Blue lights were flashing and more police cars were arriving from the direction of the gate. She could also see what looked like news crews in a line near the tower. If they'd thought to put their message on the side of the plane, they wouldn't have to go on television in Australia after all.

She throttled down with one hand and brought the altitude down with her other. How do airline pilots do this? Her brain was exploding with all the things she was having to do, it was like spinning plates, patting your head and rubbing your tummy all at the same time.

"Jacob" came Max's voice again "when we get to 500 feet, I want you to push the button marked Flaps that we talked about, right?"

"Right" repeated Jacob. He could feel his shirt sticking to his back and sweat ran into his eyes. He blinked it away. Behind him, he could hear the stewardesses telling everyone they were coming into land and to get into crash positions. Tim had buckled himself into a little seat behind him and he could hear his breathing. Beside him, Rebecca was pale. She was muttering something unintelligible under her breath.

On Max's instructions, she brought the plane down to 400 feet, 350 feet...

An alarm exploded beside Jacob. Red lights were flashing everywhere. In his ears, he could hear Maxs calm voice through all the din.

"Keep it steady, keep it steady, get that speed down, you're going too fast, keep it on line."

Rebecca pulled back on the throttle a little more and pushed down slowly with the yoke. The engine rose to a whine like a caged animal. Jacob could feel the aeroplane fighting back against them, the whole cockpit was rattling now.

250 feet, 200 feet, 150 feet.

They passed the start of the runway. They were still going too fast. Trees rushed past them in a blur, Rebecca throttled back and pushed down on the yoke.

"Not too much Rebecca. Just before you touch down, I want you to bring the nose up. Land it on its back wheels, then bring the nose down. But get that speed down NOW! Full flaps." Max was shouting now, his calm gone in the moment. They sped past the tower and all of a sudden there came a screeching and a jolt. The back wheels were down. She slammed on the brakes and smoke billowed up from the tyres. They could both smell the burning rubber in the cabin.

Rebecca pushed the nose yoke down to land the nose and suddenly there was noise everywhere. It felt as though someone had picked up the plane and slammed it into the ground. Jacob felt himself strain against the buckles of his seatbelt and in an instant, saw the front of the plane dive into the tarmac, sending up a fountain of foam.

The plane lurched forwards and started sliding sideways in the foam. Jacob slammed forwards with the impact. The last thing he saw was the instrument panel coming towards his face.

Then there was blackness.

CHAPTER NINETEEN

Jacob became dimly aware of sounds around him.

A ringing phone. A womans voice. Footsteps on a hard floor.

He felt serene as if he were floating on a cloud. In his scrambled brain, he remembered feeling like this when he was a child. Laying in a field in Yorkshire with the sun on his face. He could hear the sheep bleating far below and the bells of the village church pealing in the distance. He had nowhere to go and nothing to worry about.

A hand was on his arm. This was strange. He was on his own in a field. He could feel the hand move to his wrist and settle on his pulse. He opened his eyes slowly and winced at the light above him. A lady's face came into view above him.

"Welcome back Mr Brooks" she said in a soft Australian accent and it all came back to him in a rush. The job, the aliens, the media, the plane crash – Rebecca! He sat up and immediately regretted it as fireworks seemed to burst in his head. He groaned and thumped back down again.

"Don't try and move" the voice said again. "You've had a rough couple of days. You need to rest."

'Good plan', Jacob thought, 'Rest is good'. Then – 'couple of days?'. He forced his eyes open again. "What day is it?", he croaked.

"It's Saturday morning" the nurse said.

"Saturday?" he said with alarm. "If it's Saturday, I've got to..."

"Be an entertaining guest on my programme if you can stop lying around" said a new voice from the other side of the room. He turned his head slowly to see a tall thin man with a dazzling smile and perfect hair grinning at him. "Come on Jacob, we're going to be late if you don't get a wriggle on, get your stuff mate and come with me."

"Wha..Who are you?" Jacob managed to groan.

"Ah sorry, forgot you weren't from round these parts. I'm Chris Fairbanks, Barry's mate. The host of the tv show you're supposed to be on tonight. I can't have a gap in my schedule mate, there's not enough time to fill it. Plus you two are heroes as well as alien spotters now"

Jacob remembered Rebecca again and was about to ask when Chris continued. He got the feeling this man liked the sound of his own voice.

"Don't worry about Rebecca, she's in my car outside waiting for you, good as new." He turned to the nurse who was trying her best to be strict but seemed to have gone doe-eyed at having the tv presenter in her midst. "I know what you're going to say Nurse Bennett and I'm really sorry but I'll take great care of them okay? I've already signed the discharge papers outside, I've got a personal medic in my car and it's all good to go. Oh, and I've made a sizable donation to the hospital fund as well and that's all down to you and your care."

The nurse blushed at this; overwhelmed with his charm she started undoing the drip that was in Jacob's arm.

"Hey hang on a minute", spluttered Jacob. "What the hell happened? One moment, I was on the plane coming into land, the next I'm here? What happened to the plane? What about the passengers?"

"Calm down mate, it's all in hand. God, I thought you Brits were supposed to be quiet and reserved." He mimed a small mouse for Jacobs benefit who was not looking amused. "Stop talking and let's go. We've got a show to do. I'll tell you all about it on the way."

***

Aching from every muscle, Jacob was wheeled out of the hospital at high speed by Chris who managed to kiss a few nurses, high five the patients and sign an autograph or two on the way. He burst out of the doors with a whoop and sped towards a waiting MPV. He could see Rebecca grinning at him from the back seat and that alone made him feel slightly better but no less nauseous from the wheelchair pirouette that Chris had just performed.

He was helped out of his wheelchair, slid into the back next to Rebecca and with a short squeal of tyres they were off. With a start, Jacob noticed that Barry was in the front seat and almost cried with relief.

"Barry, you star. How are you? And Rebecca, you look fine, did I just dream all of that?"

As Barry reached over, shook his hand and handed him a much needed Coke, Rebecca filled him on the details.

The plane had landed almost perfectly. The back wheels had smacked down on the tarmac, the front nose had ploughed into the foam and they had slid along the landing strip for quarter of a mile before coming to a halt, half on the grass. Jacob had knocked himself out cold on the instrument panel in front of him, Rebecca had got mild whiplash. Tim and most of the passengers were absolutely fine. The worst injury was from a poor lady who got hit in the back of the head by a mobile phone which had flown from the hand of a thoughtless businessman three rows back.

They were now national heroes before they even managed to set foot on the ground of Australia. The Prime Minister had sent them a congratulatory message and consequently Jacob and Rebecca were now hot property. This also pleased Chris Fairbanks immensely as he had now bumped them up to top billing on his show later that evening. Bjork would now only talk for five minutes at the end and sing a shorter version of her new single.

They sped along the highway with Chris alternating between checking his watch and making phone calls to his producers every five minutes.

The driver watched the road impassively ignoring the constant chattering from his right. Jacob guessed he was probably used to it, poor guy. He could see why Barry was such good friends with the presenter. He was charm personified at all times and, while he may amplify it for the Australian public especially the female variety, he could tell it was genuine. Chris was still talking on the phone when he spotted Jacob staring at him. He flashed a dazzling smile at him whilst never pausing for breath.

After half an hour, he and Barry had completely caught up. Barry had ended up clambering over the front seat, causing shouts of alarm from the driver, and sitting between the two other Brits in the car. They were sharing out a giant bag of crisps when they heard the police siren.

"Ah, come on. Really?" Chris shouted. "What speed were you going, Bob?"

Bob spoke for the first time since Jacob had got in the car. For such a normal unassuming looking man, he had the most fantastic voice. It was as if Tom Jones' voice had got flown to Australia, and gone down ten flights of stairs to the floor marked 'Super Deep'. And then been covered in gravel.

"You told me to speed up", he rumbled. "So I sped up."

'That man needs to be in advertising' thought Jacob. Bob grumbled something unintelligible and pulled into the side. They sat and watched the policeman emerge from his car, taking his time, and walked to the open window.

He crouched down next to the open window, took a ballpoint pen from his top pocket and clicked it. Once. Twice. Three times.

"Would you step out of the car please Sir?" he said in a steady voice.

"I'm sorry officer", Bob rumbled at him – Chris turned to Rebecca and mouthed 'watch this' with an expression of unbridled delight – "but I was just trying to get Mr Chris Fairbanks back to the studio on time for tonights show."

The policeman huffed.

"If you think I'm going to believe that.." he cut off short as he spotted Chris in the front seat beaming at him. "Oh my God. It really is you."

He dropped his pen on the floor and, as he was picking it up from the floor, Chris turned back to Rebecca, raised his eyebrows and mouthed 'See?!'

The policeman reappeared at the window clutching his notepad.

"Could I trouble you for an autograph, Mr Fairbanks?" he said and held out the pad and pen. It was only now when he was leaning in that Rebecca gripped Jacobs knee and whispered "Look at his eyes."

Jacob peered at him. She was right. The policeman's eyes were alive, dancing with hidden lights. Bob and Chris had obviously not noticed any difference; he guessed it was not unusual for them. But for Jacob and Rebecca, it was terrifying. There was an alien at the window. They had seen what these things were like inside.

The policeman thanked Chris, told him he would see him tonight on telly – he never missed a show – and asked Bob to keep the speed down in built up areas. Then he was gone, back to his squad car. And, Jacob guessed, waiting for the signal to show his true self.

Bob drove off again, waving at the police car as it overtook them turning on its sirens for a couple of seconds to say goodbye. As it passed, Chris waved and then turned back to Jacob and Rebecca.

"Hey, what's the matter with you two? You look like you've seen a ghost" he said.

"Chris, that guy.." Rebecca started but Jacob cut in hurriedly. "Nothing's wrong, Chris. Just don't like getting into trouble with the police that's all."

When Chris had turned back, Rebecca looked at him with a frown. "Why did you say that? Why not warn him?" she whispered.

"He probably thinks we're nuts as it is. Remember, this isn't the guy we're trying to convince. Our message is for the scientists and people in power that might be watching. And we don't want to get thrown off the show before we've even started by outing random friendly policemen as blood sucking aliens, do we?"

"They don't suck blood"

"As far as we know".

CHAPTER TWENTY

On average, fourteen million people watched "Chris Fairbanks Talks To The Stars". When Jacob and Rebecca appeared on the show, viewing figures started off at 16 and a half million and rose to 20 million by the enforced end of the show.

A big band version of a current chart hit is performed by Chris to start the show, and it's always followed by a comedy sketch or two and then maybe a bit of stand up. It's a well worn routine that goes down well with the audience – settles them in for the talking and gets them in the right frame of mind for the humour to come. Chris likes to talk about the big issues, certainly, but there's always a rich vein of comedy running through the show. When the show had first started, it had taken time to find its feet – to find that elusive successful balance that makes every great show work – but it was on a roll now and had won numerous awards in its native country as well as being sold abroad, mostly in the southern hemisphere.

Chris had decided that he would actually start with Bjork after all for two reasons. Firstly, she was always up for a mad quote or two and had promised him that she would wear a particularly strange outfit tonight. That was always good for the headlines in the morning papers. Secondly, Jacob and Rebecca were really feeling the after effects of their accident and were recovering in the green room and getting their story straight.

Of course, their appearance tonight had changed from how it was originally billed. Instead of coming on just to talk about the white light, they were now national heroes from the plane crash and so had been granted an extra ten minutes in their slot. It was a tricky thing to be able to mould those two subjects together but Chris was confident he could carry it off and anyway he had a surprise up his sleeve for them.

As the last bars of Bjork's new single faded and the applause rose, a runner readied Jacob and Rebecca in the wings. They watched Chris as he ran through a quick summary of the air crash showing videos of the crash and the aftermath. Jacob watched film of his prone body being stretchered out of the plane and into a waiting ambulance, blood running down his face. He was shocked to see Rebecca running next to the stretcher holding his hand. He risked a glance at her but she was getting a last minute powdering of her nose.

He had lost track of what Chris was saying and all of a sudden the runner was guiding him towards the studio floor by his elbow. The lights were up, the band were playing ''Come Fly With Me' and before he knew what was going on, he was shaking hands with Chris, smiles all round. He was guided to a chair next to Chris with Rebecca next to him. The host was in the middle of the studio in a large comfy chair and there was another empty chair the other side of Chris.

The audience, who had been on their feet applauding the two British guests, settled down with the help of the host who was waving his hands in a downward motion, trying to reduce the volume so that he could start the interview.

**

In a small village near Exeter, in a large cottage that could only be reached via a long winding lane, sat Chief Alfred Brady. He had been tipped off about this television appearance by one of his staff and sat dumbfounded watching the emergence of his two former staff live on Australian television. He turned the volume up on his laptop. He had read the e-mail he had received from Jacob expanding on the white light theory and had been a little taken aback. Putting aside his anger for the way they had treated his workplace, he had to admit the theory had legs and he had already ordered a similar scan to take place this morning. He was dressed and ready to go but was sat in his kitchen glued to the computer screen to see what they had to say.

**

"Jacob Brooks and Rebecca Smith all the way from England, ladies and gentlemen!" cried Chris, and the applause started again. This time, Chris let it last a little longer until the floor manager signalled for the crowd to quieten down again.

"So just to clarify", Chris continued, "you flew halfway across the world – well, nearly halfway across the world" – he paused for laughter, perfect comic timing – "to come onto this show and tell the Australian public your theory on the white light. And on the way you manage to save a plane full of people by landing an aeroplane with not enough wheels….perfectly! Well, to that I say…Welcome to Australia! You're going to fit in nicely."

The crowd laughed and Rebecca felt it was inclusive laughter, they really were well thought of after the crash. She was hoping that may help them in getting their message across.

"So Rebecca", Chris said, "let's come to you first, tell us what you remember of that day. How did it feel knowing you were the only person on that plane that could pilot it?"

Rebecca smiled, looking to Jacob like she had been on television for years. Even with the necessary make up plastering her face, she was stunning in her beauty. They had dressed her in a simple Stella McCartney dress and all eyes were upon her.

Rebecca gave a simple and entertaining summary of the activity on the aeroplane with Jacob interjecting where he could. Chris was prompting them and throwing in a joke or two where it got too heavy. It was all going swimmingly so far thought Jacob but he was ready to get onto the white light theory as soon as possible. He didn't have to wait long.

"Now everyone thanks you for what you did to save the people of Flight 248, we really do. However, one story that is dominating the headlines as well as your personal story is the white light and you have a theory that you say"..dramatic pause.." could solve that theory and solve the mystery of that happened to Captain Phillips on the flight that you were on. Jacob, why don't you tell us what you're thinking?"

Jacob took a deep breath and met Rebecca's gaze who was smiling at him warmly. 'One chance' he thought, 'we're only going to get one chance at this'.

"Okay, well firstly can I just tell you our background quickly? We're both scientists from the Exeter Future Research Station in England specialising in..well, space stuff" he finished quickly trying not to lose the audiences interest.

"And what we're going to tell you right now might seem farfetched but it's our opinion that we know what the white light is and why it happened."

"Tell us about it Jacob" said Chris, patently trying to hurry him along to the juicy part.

"Well, in a nutshell, I ..we.." he gestured at Rebecca, "think that the white light is a distraction from an alien species. An alien species that is among us even now."

Chris nodded wisely at this but you could see the delight in his eyes as the audience gasped or tittered at this suggestion. Now that right there was a headline for tomorrow's papers already.

"Here's why.", Jacob continued, "People are going missing all across the globe. Right now. Every second. In fact, and I won't bore you with the maths or the reasons but 232 people are going missing every second. I've seen the scans from work, I've seen groups of 232 people, or what's left of them, being zapped up into space from three sources outside our atmosphere. I know it sounds crazy but.."

"When you say sources, mate" Chris interrupted, "you mean.."

"Spaceships I guess. But here's the thing. I think the white light was a distraction in order that we don't find out about these missing people. The world's media and the scientists have been talking about nothing else for days now. Nobody is listening to any other theories."

"Which is why we're here." added Rebecca.

"Which is why we're here. As well as the groups of people going up, there's groups of 232 things coming back down. Chris, people are disappearing and then reappearing. But when they come back, they look the same. They act the same. But they're actually aliens."

The audience was in hysterics now. Jacob sat up and looked at Rebecca who was frowning, puzzled and frustrated. She started to interject to help Jacob out but was stopped by Chris who held his hands up for quiet.

"Now come on people, these people are heroes and scientists, we should listen to what they have to say. Let's expand on that theory a little more here. People are going missing, right?"

They both nodded.

"And then coming back a while later, looking the same as before but they're really aliens right?"

They nodded again, wondering where this was going.

"Well, I can see where you're coming from on this. There have been people going missing. Jenson Button went missing a couple of days ago for 24 hours, there's been Michael Stipe, hey, even my deputy floor manager didn't turn up for work this morning. And she's never late - the world must be ending!"

Warm laughter again from the audience.

"But let's put this theory to the ultimate to the test shall we? Another celebrity that failed to report in to planet Earth for 36 hours earlier this week was our very own Mel Gibson. Reports said that he wanted out of his latest film due to casting clashes but there's still been no official word from the man himself. Is that because he's an alien? Is that because his ego has taken over the world? Let's find out from the man himself. Ladies and Gentlemen – Hollywood superstar – Mel Gibson!"

CHAPTER TWENTY ONE

Rebecca and Jacob looked aghast at each other. What the hell was he thinking bringing Mel Gibson on? This wasn't part of the brief. Jacob glared angrily at Barry who was in the front row and got a bewildered shrug in response. Evidently, this was Chris' little surprise and he didn't want anyone to know about it.

The tall handsome figure of Mel Gibson strode onto stage from behind Chris and shook the hosts hand warmly. He leaned in to whisper something in his ear as the audience applauded and they both roared with laughter. He then leaned across to shake a stunned Jacobs hand who was so confused he accepted the handshake without thinking. Mel went to kiss Rebecca on the cheek but she recoiled in horror as she saw the lights dancing in his eyes. It was more muted than she'd seen before, certainly a lot less than in the policeman from earlier but maybe they can tone it down if they need do, kind of like hiding their light under a bushel.

Mel frowned at the rebuff and took his seat on the other side of the host. He waved at the audience and received a wolf whistle or two for his trouble.

"Mel, mate, how are you?" said Chris.

"I'm good thanks. Excellent in fact. Just a little holiday on Mars for a couple of days and that always refreshes me."

Chris laughed and put a hand of Mels shoulder in solidarity.

"So tell us where you went then mate. One minute you were on the set of 'A Fool To Die For', your new film and the next, you apparently walked off, went home and weren't seen for 36 hours. What's the story?"

"No great drama, Chris. Apart from your good self, the media always try and come up with something more outlandish than reality just to sell papers. In the morning of the shoot, we were doing a scene where there was a lot of fighting – lots of physical action. I had been complaining about my shoulder already where my co-star Katherine Wiggins had managed to clump me with a sword. I didn't feel like continuing so went home to rest. I came back when I was fit and continued filming. That was that". He held his hands out wide to show how small a deal this was.

"But you didn't take your car?"

"No, I fancied a walk. I wandered out of the studio complex, hailed a taxi and went home."

"Well, that's fair enough I guess Mel. But we've checked cctv from the studio and there's no film of you leaving. And we've asked all the taxi firms in that area and there were no pickups from there at that time. And certainly not picking up a celebrity in full Roman gear."

"I knew you were going to say that Chris, you slippery sucker." Mel wagged a finger at him, smiling. "The papers said the same. Easy, I slipped out of the back – I was hardly going to just walk out the front entrance was I? – and then called a friend from a taxi firm I know. I know that you've rung this particular guy and asked him but he would never tell you he picked me up. Client confidentiality, you know" Mel added, tapping the side of his nose.

"So you didn't hop into a spaceship for a quick zoom around the stars then?"

The audience lapped this up.

Jacob could feel his cheeks redden in anger, they had come all this way and survived a plane crash just to be set up on live television and made fools of. He started to protest but Chris saw it coming.

"No Jacob, don't take it the wrong way. We're not making fun of your theory here, we're testing it to the limit. We've got a few alien tests for Mel to see if he really is .." cue stab of jingle music..."Human or Alien?" Applause again from the audience and this time Jacob was gratified to see

Mel Gibson look a little uncertain. He obviously wasn't given the full brief about this appearance either.

An assistant came on stage carrying a covered tray for the host. He took it from her and placed it on a small table next to his chair. There was a drum roll and Chris milked it for all he was worth, teasing the audience. The drum roll came to a crescendo and he whisked the cover off the tray to reveal several large medical instruments. The audience laughed thinking it was a joke but it was an uneasy laugh.

Mel shifted in his seat and laughed nervously.

"Hey don't go ruining my good looks with those things okay mate?"

"No, no, don't get worried. Now, I've looked on the internet to see the best way of identifying an alien and I've come up with three tests. Are you ready Mel? It'll be painless, I promise. Well, almost painless. And Jacob and Rebecca here are my independent witnesses."

The two British guests looked at each other. They had no idea whether Chris was making fun of them or cleverly trying to trap Mel into something.

Chris Fairbanks stood up.

"Right. Test number one!" he announced and picked up a small flute shaped instrument. "This is a standard issue police breathalyser. www.theyareamongstus.com state that all aliens have abnormal breath that does not comply with earth laws and it's an easy way of finding out. Mel, will you accept the breath test from Earth?"

He extended his hand towards Mel, waiting for a response.

"This is really silly Chris. You do know that, don't you?" Mel said, the humour draining from his voice. He took the breathalyser and blew steadily into it until it emitted a small beep and a red light came on. Chris took it from him, examined it and turned to camera one.

"The Alien Breathalyser Test says....you are not an alien! Or at least one who didn't have a red wine in the green room anyway."

Mel raised his eyebrows. 'I told you so' the expression said.

"Test number two!" Chris bellowed and this time the audience joined in by going 'oooh!' in the manner of a cheap game show audience. Chris started to speak and laughed instead at the absurdity of it all. He composed himself, playing for laughs. "Test number two is the infrared photograph test of doom! www.thexfilesarereal.com say that the best way of discovering an alien is to take an infrared photograph of them. Apparently the alien will reveal him or herself within the photograph. Mel Gibson, will you take the alien photograph test?"

Mel was looking seriously annoyed now.

"Look, I wasn't told about this. This is just stupid and childish. Do you really want to me do this?"

"Totally up to you, sport. It's just a photo. You told me backstage that you were looking forward to proving these crackpots wrong. Here's your chance."

The studio held its breath. The tone of Chris's voice was hard to decipher. His face was that of the usual TV host, playing for laughs and entertaining the nation but there was something in his voice that was steelier. Everyone could sense it and you could cut the atmosphere in the studio with a knife.

A pause as Mel weighed up the options then:

"Fine, take the photo."

Chris snatched up the infrared camera, asked the Hollywood star to say cheese and took the photo. In the style of an old Polaroid, the print fed slowly out of the bottom of the camera. It was bone white at first then slowly colours started to fade in to the blank square. Chris kept it facing the camera. There was a murmur from the audience and you could hear one person in the studio say "What the..".

The photo was now fully developed and showed a grumpy looking Mel Gibson starting into the camera. It wasn't the best photo in the world but showed his greying hair, his wrinkles and crows feet. However instead of his eyes, there were two burning red orbs as if his pupils were on fire. Chris almost dropped the photograph and stared at Mel. There was silence in the studio and from the watching public across Australia. In England, Chief Brady wasn't entirely sure what he was seeing. Was this all a wind-up?

Rebecca broke the silence.

"That's how you tell, Chris. It's in his eyes, look at his eyes properly, there's something – something inside them. Something not human."

"Don't be bloody daft woman", said Mel and he sat down heavily. "That's just a trick and this is a pathetic attempt to get more viewers for this excuse of a programme. Ask me some proper questions or I'm leaving. Ask me about my film- it's out in the autumn and takes place in the Civil War of.."

Chris cut across him. He was looking pale but determined.

"Mel Gibson. Human or alien? Right now, I'm really hoping human. I can cope with a grumpy alien. Will you take the third and final test. The Definitive Alien Blood Test". He held up a large syringe with a thin needle on one end.

Mel's face was like thunder. He stood up, knocking his chair backwards.

"I have starred in 35 major movies. I have pretty much singlehandedly kept the Australian film industry going for the last twenty years. I was Mad Max four bloody times. And this is the kind of treatment I get. Where's my respect?" He was shouting now.

Jacob looked across to Chris. This whole show had descended into madness and in his wildest dreams, he had never expected it to pan out like this. Chris Fairbanks however seemed to be calm personified. He had taken out his in ear speaker – Jacob guessed that the control room was shouting at him. They were still on air though and going out live. However mad this situation got, it was great telly and the producer was ordering them to keep the cameras rolling whatever happened. While Mel ranted in front of him, Chris was standing as still as a statue with the syringe in his hands. He nodded almost imperceptibly and in an instant two large security guards were by Mels side.

"What's this? You're throwing me out? You're throwing me out for getting angry? Well, that's fine, I'm going anyway. You're going to hear from my lawyers about this. You've gone way too far, mate." He delivered this last word as a stinging sarcastic rebuke in the hosts face.

The security guards moved in and held Mel's arms. However, rather than dragging him out of the studio as the audience expected, the guards wrestled him to the ground, kicking his legs away so he dropped prone and then securing his arms and legs down so he couldn't move. Mel was swearing now loudly and thrashing on the floor. Jacob and Rebecca stood up in alarm. They couldn't believe this. The floor manager ran onto the stage but was told to back off by Chris. He stood there, uncertain, before realising he was partially blocking the camera and moving to one side, off the side of the stage. Jacob caught Barry's eye in the front row. He was crying. He knew that he was probably seeing the end of his dear friends' career unravelling in front of his eyes.

Chris advanced on the struggling movie star with the syringe. He knelt down by the side of him and looked deep into the camera.

"There are probably many of you out there that think I've lost my mind and you may well be right. But I have to know."

Twenty million Australians were watching now, silent, transfixed. Bars, clubs, living rooms all across the country were hanging on every word, united in their disbelief.

"I told you earlier that these two good British people were scientists, didn't I?" he continued, still looking into the camera. "Well, I have a very close friend who works in the same field. He ran the same tests as them, he investigated what they investigated, double checked every theory that was being thrown at him like all good scientists do. And do you know what? He came up with exactly the same results. 232 people going missing every second. 232 people being returned the next day. Somehow...altered."

He wiped his brow and leant on Mel's chest who was still fighting to get up from the cold studio floor.

"I tried not to believe the whole alien thing at first. I'm not sure I still do really. Maybe I've gone insane." He laughed as if to reinforce this idea. "But I had to know. That's why I invited Mr Gibson here. The photo was my first real proof. And I don't know whether this is going to prove anything either but it's a risk I'm willing to take because if there really are things among us, among our families then I think the Australian public has a right to know don't you?"

He looked down and said softly: "This won't hurt Mel. Just stay still for me mate."

As he brought the syringe close to Mels arm, a high pitched sound started up. To Chris, it sounded like – like a jet engine or maybe a box of really angry snakes, that was more like it. Across the studio, Rebecca heard it too and let out a low moan.

Chris slid in the syringe, bringing a howl of pain from Mel. The audience were on their feet, some of them were leaving, unable to watch the scene playing out in front of them. The rest were shouting now, most people angry at how their home grown movie star was being treated, some egging Chris on to do it. The studio was in uproar.

The whining rattling noise was getting louder and Mel closed his eyes. When he opened them again, his eyes were red, a deep red that reminded Chris of congealed blood. He jumped but started to draw blood from his arm, pulling the handle back slowly.

Mel's skin sunk as if aging then melted into his face. Waves of putrid smelling skin moved across his face and Jacob shouted a warning to Chris. The host staggered backwards and there were screams from the audience. The security guards fell backs horrified and repulsed by what they were seeing. The largest of the guards scuttled backwards unable to take his eyes off the thing in front of him until he hit a studio prop wall. Then he turned and vomited over the floor.

Rebecca screamed at Chris to get away from him. The thing on the floor was getting up now and Chris stood up with him – it – to get away. The thing that used to be Mel Gibson was somehow taller now, its skin moving across its body. The eyes had sunk into the head, the hair had disappeared. The mouth had been replaced by the wide open O, lined by dozens of razor sharp teeth. The shirt on the upper half of the body had been partially ripped off where the chest of the alien had expanded and now Jacob could see the heaving bones underneath and pulsing thick veins.

What looked like gills had appeared in the chest area, a row of horizontal slits, one on either side from its neck to its stomach. They opened and closed and deep red flesh could be seen within. The eyes were dark orbs now, a single jet black pupil inside floated to the front and looked around the studio at the chaos within.

The studio staff were running for their lives now as were the audience. People clambered over each other to get to the exits to get away from the thing on the stage. An elderly lady who had come to see the show with her son was on the floor, knocked from her seat by the panicked crowd, and they were now running over her as if she were a rug. She died before she could see what her favourite film star became.

Within the crowd of people screaming and fighting for the exits were three figures. They had also come to see the show with their respective families and now they knew their time had come. It was far earlier than had been communicated but they knew that their secret was out and the order was given through the Hive command to change, to attack. The rest were coming. The three people changed slowly into their alien forms, skin melting, razor sharp teeth forming. One man, who had been holding his wife's hand only moments before now screamed an unnaturally high piercing scream and skittered away, falling over chairs and children in his way to get some distance between what him and what used to be his wife. The alien in front of him was taller now, stockier, a dirty yellow colour. The human female's skirt hung momentarily from its waist then dropped, the underwear stretching and snapping with the aliens metamorphisis.

Throughout all of this, the cameras remained trained on the stage. The cameramen had long gone, as had the control room but no one had wanted to hang around long enough to cease the broadcast and now Australia was watching the carnage live on television, uninterrupted by adverts. The camera framed the length of the stage, a wide shot. Figures ran past the camera screaming. At one point, viewers saw a man in large headphones, presumably one of the production staff, run to the lip of the stage with a microphone stand in his hand ready to attack the creature that was still standing in front of the shocked Chris Fairbanks. It turned and looked at the man with its dark eyes and he dropped his makeshift weapon and ran off camera.

Barry had also run onto the stage to join Jacob and Rebecca who were frozen to the spot. He pulled at their arms to run and shouted to Chris to get away from the thing. It had seemed like minutes but in reality, it all had taken place in less than ninety seconds.

The alien on stage turned away from the audience and back to Chris. It seemed to grin at him, its mouth elongated into a v shape and an inhuman noise came from the opening. From within the slits on its chest, things shot out and attached themselves to Chris's body. They looked to

Jacob like large slugs and he watched in horror as they slithered upwards towards the TV hosts face. Chris screamed and staggered. He tried to grab hold of one of the things but as he grabbed hold of it, it burned his flesh like acid. It was slimy and pulsing. A group of the slugs reached his neck and split off in different directions. As the viewers at home watched their favourite presenter in horror, three of the alien slugs went in his mouth, two burrowed into his ears and two up his nose. He fell now, clawing at his face, dropping the syringe at his feet. The dirty yellow alien blood glistened in the studio lights. He made a gagging noise as the things burrowed further into his face, eating at his brain.

Barry started forward, having a mad thought in his head that it was not too late to help his friend but he was held back by Jacob and Rebecca.

"We have to go Barry. Now." they shouted, and pulled him towards the stage exit. Barry cried out for his friend of many years, his dear Chris with whom he shared a love of red wine and bad jokes with. The last he saw of him as they turned to run was two more slugs feasting on his eyes, his legs drumming and jerking on the studio floor where he gained his fame and fortune he had craved so much, his heels leaving black marks on the floor.

In England, Chief Brady had dropped his morning cup of coffee on the floor. It lay there, steaming, unnoticed. He was already on the phone to work and to military chiefs explaining what he was seeing warning them of the aliens in their midst.

CHAPTER TWENTY TWO

On the long drive to the studio, Jacob had been preparing mentally for the interview. He had envisaged it going several different ways but in his wildest dreams he never thought it would go like that. In a way though, he thought to himself grimly, they had managed to realise their goal after all. As long as the camera had kept rolling and no one had stopped the broadcast then Australia now knew what they were up against and he guessed other countries would swiftly follow. The problem now was how to stop the aliens. That particular problem was not his field of expertise and he had no clue where to start.

They burst out of the studio exit door. It was still light in the evening and they had to shield their eyes from the sun directly ahead of them. The screams emanating from the studio faded as they ran towards their mpv.

"Keys", Barry shouted. "Where's the keys?"

They stopped and looked at each other. Chris had the keys. There was no way they were going to back in there.

"Try the glove box. I read somewhere that it's the place most people keep their spare key. Stupid really when you think about it, you get locked out and your spare key is.." Rebecca realised she was rambling and stopped.

"But how do we get in?" Jacob asked.

"It's unlocked I bet you." Barry said. "Chris never locked his car, he was always thinking of a quick getaway if any fans started to hassle him for an autograph, he never seemed to think someone might have actually stolen it instead."

Sure enough it was unlocked and sure enough the keys were in the glove box. Barry jumped in the driver's seat, Jacob and Rebecca next to him in the double passenger seat. He gunned the engine and they drove out of the studio gates which been left open. The security box was empty.

As they turned the corner out of the studio complex, they gasped at the sight ahead of them. People were on the streets everywhere. Cars were being packed hurriedly and children in pyjamas buckled into car seats with teddy bears thrust into their arms as they cried, having been plucked sleeping from their beds. A man and woman stood in the middle of the road having an argument about some possession or other, two suitcases at their feet with the sleeve of a shirt trailing from one of them where it had been snapped shut in a rush. As they watched from the car, the woman tore off a ring from her left hand and threw it at him, picked up her suitcase and started to jog down the street with it. As they passed the man, distraught on the side of the road now, they jumped as a creature came out of his doorway. It looked like it used to be a teenage girl, a black One Direction t-shirt hanging in strips from its engorged body. Before they could shout a warning to the man, it was on him, its large muddy yellow hands encircling his head and squeezing. They heard his cries of pain and pressed the accelerator to speed past him. They felt so helpless.

Every street was the same. People were panicking, leaving to go somewhere, anywhere, away from the horror they had seen on their televisions. Now the horror was among them. The aliens had long since abandoned their disguises and were openly attacking people. They passed an elderly lady having her throat ripped out by a creature sat on top of her, its oval mouth and rows of teeth devouring her flesh with relish. Whatever happened to 'We come in peace' thought Jacob and he shivered despite the heat.

As they sped up, another alien appeared from behind a car aiming for a teenage boy on the other side of the road. Barry swore under his breath and hit the accelerator. The car hit the creature squarely in the chest and it smacked against the windscreen leaving a yellow streak of slime. It bounced over the roof landing behind them on the road in a tangle of limbs. They screeched to a halt and all turned in their seats.

"Did we kill it?" asked Rebecca.

"I think so." replied Jacob. "It's not moving."

"But it's not foaming."

Barry looked at her, confused.

"We killed one in the research centre. It used to be our boss. I smacked it on the back of the head with a fire extinguisher and killed it. That one foamed up and kind of.."

"Fizzled away." finished Jacob. "Like baking powder. It just kind of melted into the floor."

The creature behind them twitched and staggered and lifted its body up with two heavy set arms. One of them at least looked broken, Jacob thought with relish. Its head turned towards them and the bulbous eyes settled upon them. From its chest came the slug things – it fired four of them at the car and they hit the back windscreen with a soft plop. Seconds later, there was a hiss at the acid in the things started to eat through the glass.

Barry shouted angrily and hit the throttle away from the alien in the road.

"How the hell do you kill these things? Why did that one stay down, that was worse than a fire extinguisher surely?"

"No idea mate" Jacob said, "maybe you have to get them in the back of the head. Maybe the one on the research centre was still forming – changing from Konrad to an alien and it was still weak. The only thing I do know is that those slugs are eating their way through the glass a bit quick for my liking."

Rebecca shifted over to one side as Jacob climbed into the back. The slugs were fizzing on the glass now, bubbles of acid forming around their bodies. He could see their undersides, rows and rows of tiny black blades revolving constantly and eating away anything it came into contact with. He shuddered as he thought of the two that had settled on Chris's eyes. He really hoped he had been dead by then.

He braced himself against the back of the passenger seat and kicked out with his boots, aiming for the corners and making sure to keep well away from where the slugs were located. Three kicks weakened the frame and the fourth kick send the back windscreen tumbling out of the back of the car smashing on the tarmac below taking the slugs with it. They left it behind, Barry steering the car as best he could through the increasing traffic on the side streets of Melbourne.

"We need a plan, you two" Rebecca shouted above the increased wind noise in the car. "We can't go driving around the streets all day and now we have no protection against anything that attacks us from behind. Anyone got any ideas?"

"Just the one, but it's a good one" Barry shouted as he steered round a dead body in the street. "My office"

"Your office?"

"You're forgetting where I work, dizzy girl. Melbourne Space and Science Centre. They have computers that will take your breath away, they have wonderfully talented scientists with unfeasibly large brains much like myself and the best thing of all?" He turned to Rebecca and grinned. "They have guards on the door with big machine guns."

CHAPTER TWENTY THREE

Chief Brady was locked in a grimy flat on the top floor of a tower block in Exeter. He was crouched behind an armchair that was covered in dog hair along with a teenage boy who stank of marijuana and a woman who was presumably the mother. She had tears running down her cheeks and was swearing quietly under her breath. Brady had his hand over the teenager's mouth to stop him from screaming. An alien was in the kitchen. This was not the way his morning should have gone.

An hour ago, after seeing the chaos in Melbourne via his laptop, he had called for his driver to take him into the office straight away. They had left ten minutes later and drove sedately up to his private gate leading onto the street. As he watched the electronic gate swing open, he heard a buzzing above his head and something flash across his field of vision above him. He looked up quickly but only blue sky looked back at him.

The gates opened and they turned left towards the city. It was a little over a mile to the research centre and usually took just ten minutes to get there. Brady would have been surprised if anyone suggested he could walk there in the same time. It was a hot day and the driver had his window down. This didn't annoy Brady of course as he had his privacy screen across. He turned the page of the Times and sighed. The money markets were down again.

He read the Times every day and studied the markets constantly. He had a quarter of a million tied up in stocks and shares and he was reading a very interesting article on the emergence of the Asian market when his driver was attacked by alien slugs. He was checking the share price of BT when his driver took his foot off the accelerator and collapsed sideways onto the passenger seat, a slug burrowing into his ear, gnawing on his ear drum. The car gently coasted to a stop and Brady finally became aware that something was wrong a minute later when he realised they weren't moving anymore. He lowered his paper and stared at his driver convulsing across the gear stick. He gagged and backed up onto his seat.

A creature appeared at his window, the mustard coloured eyes and floating black pupils started in at him. Brady screamed and lunged for the opposite door. He grasped the handle, fully expecting it to be locked and for the thing to crash through the window and into the back seat behind him. Thankfully, it opened first time and he tore out of the door running from the car as fast as he could, not looking back. For a large man he was moving as fast he could, half expecting the hands of that creature to reach out and grab him at any moment. He amazed himself by jumping over a small wall into a deserted children's play park and from there up a small embankment. He darted into the door of a housing complex on his left, slamming it shut behind him.

He leaned heavily against the door, panting. His heart was hammering in his chest. In the silence of the alleyway he now stood in, he could actually hear his blood rushing around his body, his heart trying desperately to keep up. He hadn't run that far and that fast since he was eighteen and his body knew it. There was a small window in the doorway and he looked through it nervously. There was no sign of anything. He hadn't imagined it though, he knew that. How many more of those things were there out there? And come to think of it, how many were in here? He got out his phone, tried to connect to the security guardhouse at the Research Centre but there was no reception. Too low down, he thought, and so he wiped his brow with his handkerchief, turned and climbed the stairs.

He met no one on the stairs and continued up, searching for that elusive first signal bar on his mobile phone. As he reached the fifth floor, it appeared – just the one bar. He dialled the number for the guard house and stood in the dim light of the staircase listening to it ring and ring.

'Strange' he thought and found the number for his assistant. The structure at the research centre was set up so that if Brady wasn't working, his assistant – a younger man called Gerald Bent – was. They mirrored working rotas and debriefed each other every time they met so that nothing was missed. He always answered his phone – he was duty bound to. Brady dialled and Gerald answered it on the third ring.

"Sir, you're alive. Where are you?" Not even a hello. Gerald was speaking quietly, urgently. He had never heard him like this before.

"Of course I'm alive. What's going on?"

"You were right about the aliens Sir. We had four of them in the centre and there's been more trying to get in. We've managed to block the area where the four where and suffered minor casualties and the guardhouse is busy trying to keep the others out. They won't die Sir. You shoot them and they go down but they get back up again Sir."

"Okay Gerald, calm down. I need to get to you, can you organise a helicopter?"

"Of course, I'll get someone out to you and bring you in, we need you here. Are you at home?"

"No, I'm in some godforsaken tower block – long story." Brady looked out the window and saw a sign outside saying Ruby Tower Hamlets. A young girl ran past the sign, screaming. He shivered despite the heat in the stairwell. "I'll text you the details. I'll try and get on the roof, just get me please and hurry."

He ended the call and started up the stairs again. That was when he heard the shuffling behind him and whirled just in time to see a creature three steps behind him, its arms already reaching out for him, mouth opening to show the deep red flesh inside. Brady acted instinctively and kicked out catching the creature square in the chest. It tumbled back down the stairs and he turned, grabbing the handrail and hoisting himself up yet another flight. He didn't look back but could hear the creature's steps once again echoing in the stairwell. He reached the top floor and, realising he didn't have time to look for the roof exit, banged on the nearest door.

No answer. He moved to the next door and banged again, hurting his fists against the rough wood, fearful that any moment now, the creature would appear behind them; he could almost feel those black pupils boring into him. He could hear voices from behind the door, hushed voices, the kind that were trying to be quiet and failing miserably. He banged again but this time there was no answer. For the second time that day, Brady found a strength he didn't know he had and kicked at the door. It rattled on its hinges but held firm. A scream came from inside. He kicked again and this time the lock broke sending the door slamming back on its hinges. He burst through and slammed it behind him.

Turning, he saw a mother with her hand over her mouth on the sofa, petrified. A younger boy, maybe seventeen, was standing in front of her with a bottle in his hands. By the looks of the glass on the rug, he had smashed it when Brady had burst it, ready to use the jagged shards of what remained in his hand on whatever was trying to get in.

"Get out. This is our place, what the hell do you think you're doing?" The boy was trying his best to sound authoritative and Brady had to admire him for that but this wasn't the time to be acting this way or handing out compliments.

"Put it down boy, I'm not your enemy. There's a creature coming this way." Brady barked. "Get behind the sofa." A person like Chief Alfred Brady hadn't got to the position he had and managed a staff of 240 every day without exuding some kind of authoritative air. When he shouted at you, you did what he said and it worked just as well on these two strangers as it did on his staff, he was pleased to note. The boy glanced at his mother and dropped the bottle on the sofa. He stepped on the seat and vaulted behind the sofa. His mother crouched down on his left and Brady settled in next to them on the right. He was grateful to see that there was a baseball bat propped up against the wall behind them next to a small mound of baseballs. He grabbed it and ducked his head down again.

The creature stumbled into the corridor. There were 7 doors ahead of it. 6 were unmarked. One was marked 'Exit To Roof – Authorised Personnel Only'. One was slightly ajar. It headed for this one and with its flabby extended arm, it pushed open the door.

CHAPTER TWENTY FOUR

The car sped towards the Melbourne Space and Science Centre knocking over another two aliens on the way. They narrowly missed an overweight man trying to run across the road with a large bundle of records in his hand. He leapt back in shock and dropped the vinyl, the black discs smashing on the road. Barry looked in the rear view mirror to see the man throw a record at the rapidly disappearing car and put two fingers up at them.

They reached the checkpoint and Barry was disconcerted to see that the barrier was up and there was no sign of any guards on duty. He was getting a bad feeling about this. They drove slowly past the checkpoint and into the main car park of the building. Most of the cars were still there and Barry glided into his marked space – Manager Only. None of them got out, there was something very wrong about this whole situation and it Barry was worried about his staff as much as himself. He had been there for seven years now and regarded the staff there as family. They worked hard and partied hard too. Last year the entire roster of staff spent New Year's Eve and Day together at work, doing increasingly mad experiments as the alcohol flowed. Barry had then rewarded them all with the first week of January off.

"Okay guys, we really need to get access to the computers in this place. I could do with finding out what's going on and trying to figure a way to end this mess. Let's stick together and pick up anything you can find on the way to use as a weapon." he said.

"Not that anything seems to kill them" Jacob replied but they did as he asked anyway and got wearily out of the car. It seemed like forever since they had last slept and couldn't imagine a future in which they would be able to sleep easily either. All of a sudden, above them came a screaming noise. They looked up. Fighter planes were streaking across the sky towards the centre of the city, the white smoke trailing behind each jet and cutting across the blue sky – the military had obviously been mobilised.

"Let's hope they have more success than we're having" Rebecca said grimly.

They moved, as a group, towards the main entrance weaving their way in between the parked cars.

The entrance was also deserted and the door swung open at their touch. Barry was gratified to see that the lights were still on. Lights meant power and power meant computers. The door swung shut behind them and the main hallway and lift were in front of them. To the right, a staircase wound its way up the side of the building. Debris and paperwork were strewn across the hallway and Jacob could see bullet holes in the wall over the lift.

"We need to get to upstairs. Room 606, sixth floor." Barry said. "That's where the main control room is and I can access every computer in the building."

"Lift or stairs?" Jacob said.

"Well, I know you're not supposed to use the lift if there's a fire. Does it count in alien attacks?"

"We need weapons first, let's check these rooms" Rebecca said and headed towards the nearest room pushing open the glass door gingerly.

Barry and Jacob stood where they were for a moment. Barry turned to his friend and said: "She's so right for you, you know. Have you told her how you feel yet?"

"You know, I'm not an expert but I'm not sure this is the right time."

"Well just make sure there is a right time eventually otherwise you'll regret it for the rest of your life."

"Well at the moment, I'm measuring that in minutes" Jacob smiled grimly and headed after Rebecca.

Every room on the ground floor was empty. No aliens, no bodies, no people.

"I've got this" Jacob said, holding up a steel rod that he had found on the floor.

Rebecca held up a fire extinguisher. "Well, this worked last time so it's good for me."

Barry grinned. "Well, I suppose I could make do with this." He held up a machine gun and strapped it round his shoulder.

The other two looked at him open mouthed.

"Where did you find that?"

"Over there on the floor. I guess someone dropped it in a hurry. I'll go first, you back me up with your small piece of metal Jacob."

They headed over to the lift and pressed the call button. It was currently showing 5 on the green LED above the doors. Jacob suddenly had the horrible thought that the lift door would open and it would be full of aliens tumbling over themselves to get to the three of them. Before he could voice his concerns to the others, the lift made a soft pinging noise and the doors slid open. It was empty.

They stepped inside and pressed the button for floor six. The door slid shut and they felt it shudder as it started to move upwards.

Rebecca leaned back against the lift wall and breathed out slowly.

"I've had enough of this nightmare. I want my old boring life back. A week ago, I was on the other side of the world trading friendly insults with this man here" – she pointed at Jacob – "while spending the rest of my time staring at bugs in Petri dishes. I miss those bugs."

Jacob nodded. "I was starting to get concerned about you and those bugs. I'm sure you started naming some of them" He shook his head sadly as if she had finally lost her mind and she grinned back at him.

Barry also shook his but for a different reason.

"Look at you two" he said, "It's so obvious you're right for each other. Why haven't you got it on yet? You know, I pride myself on being able to match make people and there's just something about you two when you're together. My mum always had a saying that I've told many people over the years, you know. She said..."

His words were cut off as the world above seemed to explode and the lift shuddered. Through the flimsy roof fell an alien landing square on Barry in a tangle of mutant arms and legs, teeth and claws. Jacob and Rebecca were knocked backwards into the corner of the lift and before they could react, the alien had fired 3 sluglike pellets at Barry's face and clamped its mouth on his neck sending a bright red stream of blood into the air and soaking the aliens head. It seemed to moan in pleasure but this sound was drowned out by Barry's gargled scream. His automatic reaction was to shoot the creature and he brought the gun round with the last of his strength and fired.

The sound of the gun going off in the enclosed space was deafening and dramatic. Bullets passed through the aliens shoulder and hit the roof; some more ricocheted off the walls and around the lift. The acrid smell of gunpowder hung heavy in the air. To Jacob, this all happened incredibly fast, faster than he could react to attack the creature himself. Another volley of gunfire went off and this time, he hit the alien in the head. Globules of thick yellow brain spattered across the lift as the head exploded. The alien body fell still and a stream of liquid streamed out of the neck of the creature and travelled in a river across the lift floor. It sizzled on the carpet tiles and ate into the fabric slowly.

Jacob leapt across to Barry who was prone on the floor. The slugs that had worked themselves into his eyes had fallen off, also seemingly dead. Jacob rolled his friend over and moaned. Barrys eyes were gone, dark holes and remnants of shredded flesh were all that remained. His face was pale and Jacob could see the bones of his skull clearly where his skin was now stretched taught. He was whispering something with the last of his breath.

Jacob leaned in close.

"code....is.....387", he heard. "for mainframe. My friend..."

His breathing stopped.

Jacob screamed in rage and frustration. The anger he felt towards these aliens was immense. They had dared to invade his home and had killed so many people. So many. And now Barry, his best friend.

He turned to Rebecca and in an instant his rage was gone. She was leaning back against the lift wall, her face a picture of shock. Her clothes were covered in blood and she had a hand held against her stomach. As he watched, aghast, she removed it and more blood poured from the bullet hole in her stomach. She tried to speak but nothing came out.

"Rebecca", he breathed and ran to her.

Behind him, the alien body twitched and started to stir. It started to lift itself up on its arms, the liquid still pouring from where its head used to be. Jacob watched in shock then came to his senses. He picked up his steel rod and slammed it down on the aliens back again and again until it lay still again. 'Not for long' thought Jacob and he looked at Rebecca again.

"I don't want to move you Rebecca but I have to. I'm sorry if it hurts."

She looked up at him fearfully with those beautiful brown eyes and his heart melted. He bent down, told her to keep a hand pressed on her wound and picked her up. She put her other arm around his neck and tucked her face into his body. Jacob stepped gingerly over the creature and pressed the button to open the door. It had stopped at the right floor, opened the door while Jacob was pummelling the alien with the rod and closed again. It opened again now, obediently, and he stepped out into the corridor taking care not to bang Rebecca's head on the frame. He checked left and right but the coast was clear. In front of him was a large office not unlike the main control room back in Exeter. The entire office was protected by thick glass and there was a large entrance door set into the far wall. Next to this door was a small panel with a numbered pad. Jacob walked to this now and punched in 387, Barry's last contribution to this world.

The door swung open with a hiss and Jacob staggered inside. Among the many banks of computers, printers and scientific equipment were several large sofas clustered around a whiteboard. He gently put Rebecca down on a sofa, wincing at her cry of pain and sat next to her softly. He stroked her hair and she looked up at him.

"It hurts Jacob, it feels like someone ripped my insides out." Coughing now and wincing with the pain, she continued "I don't want to die."

"You're not going to die. Not now. Not here."

She was grateful for the steely confident tone in his voice. Right now, it was exactly what she needed.

"Wait here, I'll be back in 2 minutes, let me see what I can do." he said and went over to what looked like the main computer. He turned it on, typed in Barrys name and for a moment, was stumped when it asked for a password. Then he tried "Merlot" and he was in. Typical Barry. He fought back tears again thinking of his friend he had to leave behind.

Quickly he logged into the mainframe and searched for medical supplies. Room 18 on the first floor. He accessed cctv and requested first floor hallway cameras. His eyes widened as he saw a large group of aliens in the hallway. He could count at least 14 – no idea what they were all doing there but it was fairly obvious that he wasn't going to be able to get near the medical room. Stumped, he breathed out heavily before having a stroke of inspiration. He searched for nearest medical facilities and got the following result:

Newcross Hospital Melbourne

0.3 miles W

2 minutes walking distance

'Two minutes?' he thought 'but that's got to be...' He ran over to the window facing to the east and saw a sight that rose his spirits. The hospital was right across the road. But if he couldn't get out of the main entrance then..

"The staircase" said Rebecca reading his thoughts.

He stared at her then behind him where she was shakily pointing. Of course, the main staircase for the building was on the outside of the building. It led all the way down to the ground floor and was encased entirely in glass so he could see if anything was coming and more importantly if anything was waiting for him at the bottom. Of course, any hostile things could also track his progress down to the ground but he would have to deal with that as best he could. He had to get help for Rebecca. There was no other option; he couldn't lose her.

He went back to her now and knelt next to her. Their eyes met, both brimming with tears.

"I won't be long. The door's completely secure. I'll get help. I promise you, I won't let you down."

"I know you won't." She said, gripping hold of his hand hard. She looked from his eyes to his lips and before he realised what was happening, she was softly kissing him. It was everything he had ever dreamed of and for a moment he forgot everything and was lost in the moment. She broke away gently and held his astonished gaze, smiling warmly at him despite her pain.

"Come back and save me" she whispered and pushed him gently away. He staggered to his feet, still dazed then remembered where he was and what he needed to do. He picked up his steel rod, strode to the exit door and, without looking back, opened it and disappeared down the staircase.

CHAPTER TWENTY FIVE

The alien stepped into Room 240 and scanned the room. Nothing. It moved into the main lounge and looked at the human habitat. The things that humans liked to keep. The human food on the table. It looked to its right and went into the kitchen seeking out the humans it knew were in here.

There was a movement behind it and before it had time to turn or attack, a human was there striking it.

Chief Brady brought the baseball bat down on the thing in front of him in the kitchen. Falling forward, its outstretched limb scattered a pile of plates. They exploded on the hard tiled floor and the alien fell with them; it tried to turn to see its assailant but Brady brought the baseball bat down on it again and again until it fell still. A final blow to the head saw its distorted face slew to the right, the bones in its skull crushed under the onslaught.

He grabbed his phone and called the Research Centre again. Again Gerald answered three rings in.

"Sir" he said

"Where's the helicopter. I've two others I need to evacuate."

"It's on its way Sir – two minutes on the roof. You'll need to be quick though Sir, we've had reports of large gatherings of aliens all around your area"

Brady snapped closed his phone and turned to the stunned family behind him.

"Come on" he said holding out his hand to the mother "We need to go – now."

They didn't move, their eyes flicking from the man who had kicked down their door and was now covered in alien blood to the alien creature itself out cold on their kitchen floor amongst their recently washed up dinner plates smashed all round it.

"Now!" Brady shouted and this seemed to jolt them into action. As the teenage boy passed the alien it twitched sending a jolt of speed into his movements. They hurried through the door and into the corridor checking both ways for any further surprises.

As they approached the roof exit door, Brady could hear the approaching helicopter and quickened his pace. He slammed through the emergency exit and heard an alarm wail somewhere behind him.

"W-Where are we going?" said the mother.

"Somewhere safe" Brady said, "Somewhere without aliens. That good enough for you?"

She smiled for the first time and it lit up her face as the chopper landed in front of them.

"Perfect", she said.

**

As they flew over the city, the mother hugging the son tight, Brady saw the full extent of their problems.

He looked down to see streams of aliens in the streets; it was now hard to see any humans around at all. He guessed they were either hiding or dead. He wondered how they had managed to get so many soldiers on the planet at once seeing as though they were only replacing 232 at a time through the streams as Jacob had told him in his e-mail. Then he saw his answer. In the main square of the city centre sat four squat black ships. Three more were on the main roads into the city and he could see odd ones here and there as they flew over. They had obviously abandoned the streams and come in full force. He assumed the streams were just there to get their troops on the ground surreptitiously but when they were discovered then what's the point in hovering above the Earth; they had just landed the whole fleet. After all, what's to stop them? He looked for any military intervention but could see none; perhaps the takeover had been too swift, even for them.

"Are you okay?" he shouted to the mother in front of him over the din of the rotors. She said nothing but nodded. She too had seen what was in the streets and the terror was etched on her face. They had all seen enough to give them nightmares for months but it wasn't over yet.

They landed in the large courtyard of the Research Centre. The building was still secure and Brady had seen the guards managing to keep the aliens at bay from their guard posts but he wondered how long they could last for.

Leaving the two guests inside the helicopter, he ran inside the Research Centre accompanied by a guard. He made his way to his office nodding to colleagues on the way, putting a supportive hand on shoulders where he could see panic in people's eyes. He closed the door behind him, turned on the computer, patched into the building intercom and spoke; his voice rang clear through the centre.

"Ladies and Gentlemen, your attention please. I repeat, your attention please. This is Chief Alfred Brady speaking. I have worked in this building for over twenty years and every single day someone different makes me proud. Someone different every day makes me excited about science all over again. Today, we face our greatest challenge. Today, I need every single person in this building to make me proud. Delve deep inside yourselves. Think about how good you must be to work for this centre and what you can do for mankind today. I want you to help each other, work fast and work hard and let's find a solution to this challenge that is facing us. Let us do this today so that we can all face a better tomorrow. Brady out."

He clicked off the intercom and slumped back in his chair, spinning it round so that he looked out of his office window and across the city. Smoke rose from high rise buildings and black spacecraft hovered menacingly on the skyline. He hoped beyond all hope that his little speech made some difference because he was certainly out of ideas himself. He poured himself a drink from the bottle of whisky that he kept in his drawer and closed his eyes.

CHAPTER TWENTY SIX

Jacob was also discovering the black ships engorged with aliens. He watched from halfway down the staircase as one landed half a mile away, let out all its soldiers and flew off again with a low hum. He slunk down the stairs, trying to hide as much as possible when he was fifty feet up and surrounded by glass.

The hospital was just over the road. He estimated that he could reach it in a minute and a half if he ran to the main entrance but that was ninety seconds in the open with only a steel rod for protection. Where were the military? Had Earth really been overrun that quickly? Carefully, he opened the staircase door and squeezed through the gap running over to the corner of the research centre building. Peeking round the corner, he could see three aliens at the end of the street – sentries? One more was at the other end but appeared to be eating something on the ground. Or someone. There was no way he could get across with those three there. Just a few steps into the road and they would see him. He looked desperately for anything around him that could help him in his cause but there was nothing. He was trapped.

Then for the first time that day, fate lent a hand. From round the corner shot a jeep. Two men were in it, dressed completely in camouflage and screaming at the top of their voices. They both had shades on and bottles in their hands. They were driving directly at the aliens and Jacob watched open mouthed as they drove straight into them before they even got a chance to attack. Two of them went flying over the bonnet of the jeep and the other managed to step out of the way. This remaining one pointed at the jeep with one hand and Jacob watched in horror as a thin beam of what looked like mucus shot out of its finger and onto the back of the jeep. It hit the metal and immediately started eating into it demolishing the exhaust and tow bar within seconds and advancing rapidly towards the two men who hadn't even noticed.

The driver slammed on his handbrake and span the jeep round in a perfect semi circle leaving black tyre marks on the tarmac. Jacob could see the mucus working its way over the back seat now eating everything in its path but he guessed that the two occupants were too drunk to notice. The passenger stood up now and produced a bazooka – where the hell had he got that from? As the two aliens in the road staggered to their feet to rejoin their colleague, the man in the jeep screamed something unintelligible at them – he sounded French – and fired. The missile connected in a millisecond and struck the middle alien in the chest blowing him to pieces. The other two were blown apart as well sending pieces of dark yellow flesh scattering across the road. With a laugh, the driver tried to turn the jeep but belatedly realised he had no back wheels. The mucus was eating through their seats and they jumped out in a panic landing heavily on the floor and then running off up the street away from Jacob. He looked back down the street to the other alien but there was no sign of it.

Taking his chance, he ran across the road and into the hospital. An ambulance was on its side embedded in the large plate glass window. Jacob could see two bodies inside covered in blood – it looked like one patient and the paramedic. He gingerly looked inside but it looked as though all the medical supplies had already been taken by someone. He picked up a scalpel though and made his way inside the hospital. It was a mess. Equipment and bodies were strewn everywhere. Where on earth should he start? He checked the floor map on the wall and guessed at accident and emergency. Down the corridor and three rooms in.

Carefully making his way through the wreckage, he kept his eyes peeled for anything that was not human. Even so, he almost missed the small boy in the corner.

He had reached the A&E department and was just looking around to find the medical supply room when he heard a sobbing. He immediately pointed the scalpel ahead of him with his outstretched arm and walked slowly towards the sound. It was coming from behind a curtain and he briefly thought of the film Psycho as he approached it, knife in hand, ready to strike at the figure behind it.

He ripped the curtain back to see a small boy there crouched in the corner. He figured he was about six or seven dressed in jeans and a stripy t-shirt with a rabbit on the front. His dark hair was sticking up wildly and there was a dark patch on his jeans where he had wet himself. He was breathing very raggedly and sobbing, tears running down his face. Jacob dropped the knife at his feet in shock.

"Hey buddy" said Jacob, crouching down. "Where's your mum and dad?"

The boy's chest heaved and his eyes closed in pain. Jacob guessed where his mum and dad might be and only hoped that the small child didn't get to watch it.

"Can't breathe", the boy said. His voice sounded like it was being squeezed out of him through a tight tube and he put a hand up weakly in front of Jacobs face. He made a fist then extended a finger and waved it up and down. It took a moment before Jacob suddenly realised that he was miming something.

"What is it buddy? Are you choking?"

"asthhh..." he gurgled.

"Oh God, asthma? Is that what you've got? Asthma?"

The boy nodded and again mimed with his fist. 'He's miming an inhaler', Jacob suddenly realised and looked around him wildly. 'Okay', he thought, 'asthma inhaler and stuff for Rebecca. Get on it Jacob'.

He laid a hand against the boys cheek and winked.

"Back in a minute mate – hold on."

He got up, his knees cracking. Locating the medicine room, he looked around for the stuff he needed. It had been looted already and unrolled bandages were covering the floor. Packets of drugs had spilled onto shelves below and he threw packs around trying to see the shelf labels. Eventually he found it. In the corner, by a large bottle of green murky liquid, was a box marked Inhalers. He grabbed it and slit open the tape sealing the box. Jackpot. There was a whole bag of readymade inhalers here that were just waiting for the prescription labels to be added onto them and given out. He grabbed one and gave it an experimental puff. It gave a gratifying puff of whatever gunk was inside these things and Jacob turned to go back to the boy.

As he came out of the room, he checked both ways in the hallway for anything coming. Still deserted; his luck was holding here. When he got back into the A&E department, he realised he had jumped the gun a little on that thought and realised his terrible mistake. Why did he not think to bring the boy with him?

An alien was feasting on him. He could see the boy, still alive, screaming silently and the creature clamped onto his thigh, the revolving teeth boring into the meaty flesh within. Its hands were on the boys stomach clawing at the skin there trying to find a way through to get to the intestines. What were these monsters? Without thinking Jacob ran towards them both as fast as possible and kicked out at the alien. His boot connected with the side of its head and it screamed a high scream which seemed to come from the alien and from everywhere in the room at the same time. It fell off the boy and started to scramble to its feet again.

Jacob realised with a dull start that he hadn't got the scalpel anymore, what had he done with that? The creature came at him now, groggily, advancing quickly. Jacob grabbed a plastic chair that was next to him and threw it at the alien. It bounced off its chest and it seemed to grin at him with its horrific flesh filled mouth. He threw another and another, they slowed the creature slightly but it was still coming at him and he realised with horror that he had backed himself into a corner. There was nothing here but a cork notice board on a wall advertising local charity events. He tried to rip this off the wall to use as a weapon but it held fast.

The thing was six feet away now and the slits in its chest widened. Jacob knew what was coming – he remembered the full horror of what had happened to Chris on the studio floor – and pressed himself back into the wall clenching his fists tight. His right fist suddenly hurt and he realised he was still gripping the inhaler. Using the only thing available to him, he brought the inhaler up in front of him and puffed it into the aliens face – three times in quick succession, his face turned to one side and eyes screwed up ready for the inevitable attack.

The effect was dramatic.

As the spray from the inhaler hit the alien, it seemed to fold in on itself like a piece of paper being screwed up. Its dark yellow eyes rolled back and the mouth snapped shut and melted into its own head. There came a piercing whistling sound like a kettle and it crumpled in front of Jacob who had opened his eyes now and looked down at the collapsing form in front of him with a look of shock. The body on the floor now started to bubble and foam and a putrid smell rose from the alien's corpse making him want to vomit. The piercing sound lowered in tone gradually until it seemed to turn into a growl. Then it stopped; silence was absolute.

Jacob looked at the mess at his feet. He realised he wasn't breathing and that his muscles were still tensed; he breathed out a long breath and relaxed his body, blinking back tears. He felt like crying there and then and struggled hard to keep his sanity. The things he'd seen today nearly sent him over the edge. He looked past the alien to the small boy still slumped in a corner, his leg now completely red from the blood oozing streaming from his tiny body. Jacob stepped carefully over the creature, making sure he didn't step in any of the bubbling liquid, and ran over to the body. His arms were over his head, his hair flopping over his face. Jacob reached out a hand, grabbed his shoulder and pulled, turning the boy over to lay on his back. His eyes stared glassily up at the ceiling and his mouth dropped open. Jacob felt the tears coming now, he couldn't help it. He cried for this boy, for his parents that were probably already dead, for all the victims out there that were being picked apart by these uninvited creatures. Most of all, he cried at the sheer waste of it all – so many victims, so much blood being spilled. His tears fell onto the boy's chest and Jacob muttered "I'm sorry".

He wiped his eyes on his sleeve and sat up looking upwards towards the ceiling to try and stop the stem of tears. Suddenly his mind was full of vengeance. He would stop this. Nobody tried to take over his home planet and got away with it. He grinned at the memory of the alien dissolving in front of his eyes and realised he could well have a weapon. He stared down dumbly at the inhaler, a tiny plastic thing full of a cocktail of unknown chemicals. Could it be that this piece of medical equipment, designed to save lives, was exactly the thing to kill these invaders – to cause them untold pain and suffering. He hoped so – he remembered Chris, Barry, the people he had seen in the street being attacked, the untold number of victims. God, he certainly hoped so. He remembered Rebecca again then and was stirred back into action.

Pausing only to close the eyelids of the small boy – 'I never even knew your name' he thought sadly – he went back to the medicine supply room. Spying a bag on the lower shelf, he filled it with inhalers, fifty or more. He scanned the shelves for something that would help Rebecca and decided on bandages, antiseptic wipes, morphine and paracetamol. He shoved them all in the bag, grabbed a fresh inhaler in his fist and ran for the exit. No more aliens impeded his exit and within a couple of minutes he found himself at the hospital main exit staring across at the glass staircase leading back up to the main staircase and Rebecca. Sitting squat on the tarmac between where he stood and the staircase was an alien spaceship.

CHAPTER TWENTY SEVEN

The ship sat squarely in the middle of the road fifty feet from him. As far as Jacob could see it was hexagonal in shape. There were no markings anywhere on the black surface of the ship but panels dotted the sides and lower half. It was supported by thick black legs with pads stretched out as if gripping the surface. It looked incredibly powerful, even just sitting there motionless it was exuding a feeling of power. It made no noise. On the side facing down on the street, to the spaceships left, a door was open and a ramp had been extended to reach the road. This reminded Jacob of E.T. and a thousand other space movies and he smiled to himself thinly, despite the gravity of the situation.

As far as he could see though, there were no sign of any aliens. Of course, that didn't mean they weren't there. He could sneak past the ramp and they would all be sat there in the ship's entrance chewing the fat. He could imagine them all turning as one to watch him walk past their view and moving toward him, over him, eating his battered body. No. He couldn't sneak past the ship. He couldn't hide in the hospital, Rebecca needed him. For all he knew, she had bled out up there, dying all on her own with the taste of his lips on hers being her last comforting thought.

He knew his only option but that didn't mean he liked it. He reached into his bag of medical supplies and brought out a handful of asthma inhalers. Shoving two each in his pockets, he put two more on the ground in front of him keeping a wary eye on the ship in front of him for any sign of activity. He screwed up the medical bag and jammed it into his inside pocket before picking up the two inhalers in front of him. He hoped this would work; this was going against everything he was used to in his scientific background. He was always trained to formulate a theory and test every variable until you were sure that the results you were getting were correct. Or to put it a more scientific way – until you were mostly sure that you were correct; there were never any guarantees in science. He was now basing his theory that he could cause harm to aliens on one incident only. For all he knew, that particular alien could have a specific allergy to the chemicals he was packing in the tiny plastic tubes he now gripped in his sweaty fists. It could have been ill and therefore weakened. A million different variables could have affected that outcome of that particular situation. He was now going to test that theory by walking into a spaceship and taking on whatever he found in there. He was doing this, he told himself, for three reasons. The first was so that he could clear his way back to Rebecca. The second was to test his theory out. If it worked, then he needed to spread the word. The third reason was that right now, with everything he'd been through and with everything these creatures had done to him and the people he loved, he wanted to exact some sort of revenge. And if they were all going to die eventually in this invasion, he wanted to take a few of them out with him before they managed to get him. He wasn't sure which of these reasons was pushing him on the most but decided it didn't matter. He was wasting time and he needed to get this done. Getting to his feet, he strode towards the ship.

He walked purposefully towards the ship checking either side as he went. His entire mind was concentrated on that doorway, that ramp. However as he got closer, he noticed two things. Firstly, he was that, as far as he could see, the ship was deserted. Secondly, the angle he was looking at the ship from his vantage point in front of the hospital made it look as though there was no way past to the entrance. Now that he was nearly able to touch the ship, he could see a way through and he suddenly changed his mind, darting across the back of the craft and into the staircase, grasping the handle tight, twisting the knob violently and lurching breathlessly into the doorway. He span round, expecting to see a furious squad of alien soldiers following him but there was nothing. He was lucky.

He turned again and took the stairs two at a time, visions of Rebecca filling his mind. He reached the top and burst back into the research centre.

"Rebecca" he shouted and saw her on the sofa, right where he had left her. She was motionless, on her front facing away from him, one arm hanging down and the hand limply resting on the carpeted floor. Her skin was pale and blood soaked the sofa from her waist down. He had wasted so much time in the hospital. Was he too late?

He ran across to her and fell to his knees next to her, barely feeling the blood soaking into his jeans. He carefully brushed the hair away from her face and, to his utter joy, she opened her eyes slowly saying his name quietly. He kissed her then on her cheek, out of relief. She managed a small smile and closed her eyes again.

Retrieving the medical bag from his pocket, he took out the morphine and syringe. He suddenly realised that he had no idea how much to give her and grimly realised the irony of saving her life only to kill her with an overdose of drugs. There were no instructions. He loaded half the syringe and tested that it worked by holding it vertically and spraying some of the painkiller in the air. He wasn't sure what this achieved but doctors always did this in the movies so he dutifully followed suit. Warning Rebecca first, he found a vein in the crook of her arm and slid the fine syringe in. She jerked slightly as the needle pierced her skin but kept still as he slowly pushed the plunger down, realising the liquid into her bloodstream. When he had finished, he removed the syringe slowly until it was clear of her arm leaving a small pearl of blood on her pale skin. He took a plaster from the box he had brought from the hospital and sealed the tiny wound. Then he found the rubbing alcohol and bandage and located the bullet wound in her side. As far as he could see, there was only one entry wound and it was close to the edge of her body rather than further in where her vital organs lay. He was guessing of course, but he was hoping against hope that this was what they called a flesh wound. He wiped as much of the blood away as he could, and put his arm under her body to lift her up slightly. Then he wrapped the bandage around her as best he could and tied it tight with a crude knot. She did not stir as he moved her and he assumed that the morphine had kicked in already. He checked her breathing – shallow but regular. That was good. Sleep was healthy.

There was nothing else he could do now for her now except let time take its course and try and get professional help in the meantime.

He stood and stretched, extending his arms to the ceiling and flexing his fingers. His spine cracked and he lifted himself up onto his toes. Then he relaxed feeling some of the tension drain from him. Walking to the window, he watched black smoke drift lazily up from a building about a mile away. A spacecraft flew through the column of smoke sending it swirling in different directions before resuming its lazy ascent to the sky. He thought of all the people left out there in the city, across the world, that were under threat from these beings and he was suddenly overwhelmed with guilt. He had potentially discovered a weapon; something that would finally kill these creatures – and fast. But did it? Again, he thought back to his scientific basics. One successful trial on a live alien didn't constitute a weapon that would help mankind fight back.

He looked back at Rebecca, sleeping soundly on the sofa, her legs drawn up to her chest and realised what he must do. It was the last thing in the world he wanted to do but he knew the responsibility rested squarely on his shoulders.

He had to go and find an alien. And kill it. And if his asthma inhalers didn't work..... Well, he didn't even want to think about that possibility. He walked back to Rebecca, kissed her on the cheek again gently and then went through his pockets again to check his stash of inhalers. He gave each of them an experimental puff just to make sure they were full. The last thing he wanted was to go face to face with these things and find he had a bag of duds.

He was surprised now at how he felt. He should, by all rights, be nervous and those butterflies in his stomach were definitely there making their presence felt but it was more excitement than anything. Layered over this strange feeling was a steely resolve. This action may be the last thing he ever did on this planet. Or it may be the beginnings of the fight back for mankind. Either way, he was doing it for Rebecca. She was the best thing to happen to him for years and he wasn't going to give the chance to make it work without a fight.

He walked towards the window again, looked down towards the ground to make sure the ship was still there and opened the door to the staircase once more. Again, he walked down carefully, an inhaler in each hand. At every turn, he checked below him and stopped, listening for any signs of activity. He certainly didn't want to be surprised by something when he could have avoided it by being careful. He reached the bottom with no dramas and twisted the doorknob to open the door. He pulled it open, walked through and turned to close the door behind him quietly. Then he checked both ways along the street to see if anything was there. Apart from the ship, what was left of the jeep and a few empty parked cars here and there, it was still deserted.

The entrance to the ship was thirty feet away facing slightly away from him. He marvelled at it. It must have been at least eighty feet across and forty feet high, completely black. He wondered how on earth it could fly as it gave the impression of being totally solid. He quickened his pace and made it to the ramp in less than thirty seconds. Jumping onto the ramp, he peered inside. Blood pumped wildly through his veins, his heart hammered in his chest. His calm was gone now and he felt an urge to just turn and run; to get away from this inhuman thing as fast as possible. Fight or flight he guessed. 'Time to fight' he told himself and started up the ramp.

He could see nothing inside the ship, only a dull red light. When he reached the top, his view didn't improve. Instead of the hordes of soldiers his mind was expecting, he could just see a hazy red glow. Gripping his inhaler tight within his fist, he willed himself to take a step forward, then another, until he was inside the craft. More red haze. He took another step forward and couldn't help himself from crying out as his body and face hit something wet. He gagged as it seemed to envelop his face and press into him; he tried to step backwards but it held him fast. Realising the only option was to go forward, he lurched in that direction and fell free of whatever it was that was covering him. He landed on his knees and got up hurriedly looking behind him.

The door had gone and he could no longer see the outside world. In its place was that same red haze. He turned and looked around him. A corridor stretched a short distance in front of him and then turned off to the left. The walls and ceiling were jet black and smooth with some kind of thick liquid running down and across them. He continued forward, still hearing nothing. Turning the corner, he saw another corridor that seemed to stretch for a mile in front of him; he could hardly see the end. How was that possible? He was very aware that he was now trapped inside with no idea of where he was going or how to get back out. If those things returned en masse, he was in deep trouble.

He took a few more steps down the mile long corridor and felt the same wet feeling of the invisible barrier clutching at his body and face. He pushed through this time and the corridor in front of him disappeared to be replaced by a large room with bright yellow lights shining down from the ceiling. Jacob counted seven large screens around the room, all showing parts of the city and the alien soldier's activity. They shone blue light into the room and illuminated a figure standing on a small plinth in the middle of the room facing away from Jacob. It was holding its arms up in front of itself, fingers extended and what looked like beams of thin energy was streaming from the fingers to the edges of two of the screens on the far side of the room. It was a tall creature, Jacob guessed at seven feet, and its head was bulbous, grotesquely oversized in relation to its slender muscular body. The skin was deep yellow and wet, rivers of liquid running constantly over the skin.

Jacob shrank back into the corner of the room but as he did so, it seemed to sense his presence. The beams from its fingers stopped and it turned slowly toward him. The face of the creature made him recoil in horror. It seemed to Jacob that every human face was being worn by the alien at once. His mind reeled. As the creatures expression changed from shock at having company in its lair, to anger and eventually settling on what looked like a gentle humour as it looked at Jacob, the face shifted from one recognizable human face to another – a black lady was the shocked face, and elderly man was anger and a middle aged man with a red birthmark on his cheek was the gentle humour. The horrifically unsettling aspect of it was that each face had the pain filled eyes of the human. The expression now may be gently amused but the eyes were screaming at Jacob, they were filled with pain and anguish and looked as though they were burning in the fires of hell that very moment. It made Jacob feel sick.

It was time to make this thing pay. He ran forward; there was about ten feet between him and the creature and he covered it in less than two seconds. Holding the inhalers up in front of him, he pressed down on the tops sending out puffs of chemicals. It looked so inconsequential against the mass of the thing in front of him but he remembered what it had done to the thing in the hospital. He was right up against it now, inches away from that wet body and he used both inhalers on that skin. But nothing was happening. The chemicals seemed to form a cloud just in front of the skin but never quite get there. It was being stopped by some kind of force field. He stared in horror and then looked up.

The alien was looking down at him and he realised why there had been an expression of humour. It knew there was nothing he could do to hurt it. Its expression changed again now to concentration – a teenage girl etched on the face, about seventeen years old, pretty, but those eyes of pain again – and Jacob suddenly felt as though he had been hit by a large invisible hammer. He flew across the room, slamming into the wall and slumped down on the floor. He had almost been knocked out but not quite. He blinked to get his senses, felt the back of his head and his fingers came away wet. He brought them round so that he could see – he was bleeding from the back of his head. The blood looked almost green in the strange light.

He got to his feet groggily and realised he didn't have a backup plan. Clearly the inhalers didn't work and now he was trapped inside the control room of a spaceship with this murderous thing. He knew in an instant that he was going to die here, smashed to pieces by this creature.

Now he felt a new feeling. Inside his mind, there was a kind of tickling, like someone was trying to prise open the edges and get inside. He stared up at the creature again and the amused expression was back; that scared him. His mind was light headed, he could see the alien in front of him but there were shapes in front of his eyes obscuring his vision. He blinked hard and fingers probing his mind forced their way in, he felt his mind flip and now he had the peculiar experience of looking at the creature in front of him whilst also simultaneously looking back at himself. The thing was in his mind. He panicked and clutched at his head, screaming in a high girlish voice. He tried to back further away from the centre of the room and his feet scrambled on the floor trying almost to climb up the wall behind him. In his mind, he saw himself scrabbling on the floor, his hands on his head, his wild panicked eyes bulging and bloodshot.

Then the voice came inside his mind. It was like a rusty saw tearing into the soft tissue of his brain and he must have been screaming but he couldn't hear himself anymore. He could just hear the voice. It was saying just one word.

VICTORY

VICTORY

VICTORY

It tore into his brain time and time again and Jacob writhed on the floor knowing he was nearing the end of what his body could take. The pain was hitting him like a sledgehammer every time the thing spoke; it felt like its hands were squeezing his brain like a clamp. He forced open his eyes to a slit and saw the creature grinning at him. Its teeth glinted in the yellow light. He was going to die on this floor.

From out of nowhere, an image of Rebecca filled his mind. She was smiling up at him just after they kissed for the first time. Her eyes sparkled and shone like diamonds in the sunlight and her blonde hair lay across her forehead gently. Her image gave him strength and he felt the grip on his mind stutter. He concentrated solely on the image of Rebecca and she mouthed a word at him. In his mind, the word got louder and louder.

no

No

NO

He was shouting it inside his mind now; the Rebecca image inside his head was shouting the word and together they became stronger. He opened his eyes and saw the alien looking down at him in fury. Jacob summoned the last of his strength to do two things. Firstly he grinned at the alien and for the first time outside of his own brain shouted the word 'NO'. Secondly, he brought up an inhaler to his mouth and pressed the top down releasing the chemicals into himself. He pushed down again and again. The chemicals flew down his throat, into his lungs, into his bloodstream. They were carried along his veins and in seconds had hit his brain which was still connected to the creature which, in turn, was connected to the alien soldiers that had come from that ship and were patrolling the neighbourhood.

It didn't have the same impact as earlier in the hospital but it gave Jacob the advantage. He felt the grip on his mind suddenly release and his mind snapped back into his own. The alien staggered on its plinth, its grotesque head pulsating and it let out an enraged scream. It raised its hand again now to attack, to send a stream of energy towards Jacob and to blow him to bits right where he stood. But Jacob was faster. He shoved his hands in his pockets, brought out two new inhalers filled with the toxic chemicals and raced towards the creature. The force field was gone now, destroyed when he had destroyed the connection. He lunged toward the alien, crashing into that wet flabby body and pushed the inhalers down again and again into its face and body. It screamed and Jacob felt like his ears were going to burst. The body began to bubble and foam as it thrashed on the floor under Jacob and he rolled off as the skin melted in on itself; the scream dying out as the creature disappeared into a thick yellow foam that smelled like a thousand rotting animals.

Jacob was covered in it and he staggered to his knees then vomited where he was, heaving every last scrap of half digested food from his stomach. He rolled onto his side and lay there, panting. Some kind of connection must have still been evident, as he knew – he didn't know how but he just knew – that the alien soldiers outside were dead. It was the connection they had with this ship. The chemicals had entered the alien here and flooded out in a mental connection to the alien passengers on the ship. They had dropped where they stood, screaming as their skin had burned and bubbled, their dark orb-like eyes revolving back in their heads and collapsing in on themselves. As Jacob lay on the cold floor of the ship, he instinctively knew that they were all dead. They had been stationed in a three mile radius of the city and now they were all gone. That gave him a chance.

Again, it was the thought of Rebecca that stirred him into action. She was waiting for him. He stood up slowly and turned around, his back to the screens. He expected to see the back wall of the ship but instead saw the fading light of the street outside, the exit, the ramp leading down into the street. Whatever had been barring his way into the craft was now gone, and Jacob made his way back outside, his legs like rubber. He grinned weakly as he saw four pools of froth outside; the connection was weakening as he left the ship but he knew that these aliens had been summoned by the master one inside. They died outside in agony as the rest had done.

The fresh air outside made his stomach feel a little better. His strength was returning and his mind was his own again. He had a weapon. There was a way of fighting back against these things. He ran back to the staircase and made his way back up to Rebecca.

As he reached the top and burst through the door, he was surprised to see her sitting up. She was still deathly pale, her hair stuck to her face with sweat, but she was alive and smiling weakly at him. He sat down next to her and neither of them spoke. They didn't need to – this was a different type of mental connection but just as powerful. They gazed into each other's eyes and finally embraced.

It was Rebecca that broke the silence.

"Where have you been? Tell me what's happened." Her voice was weak but she was desperate to hear what he had gone through. She could see something in Jacobs's eyes that told her she needed to hear his story.

He explained his discovery in the hospital watching her shed a silent tear as he told her about the small boy. He stopped talking, meaning to ask her if she was okay, but before he could she tapped his knee and nodded urging him on, her eyes shining with tears.

When he had finished, she was looking at him wild eyed with wonder.

"So we can beat them? What is this stuff in here?" and then "We need to be back at work. Maybe they can manufacture this mix of chemicals – we need to drop it everywhere. Call work, Jacob. Now." She shouted the last word then doubled up in pain, tears springing from her eyes.

Jacob held his hand to her cheek and felt the warmth of her skin.

"I will. As soon as I can. But you come first, I need to get you to a doctor."

"No, I'll be..." she cried out in pain again and clutched her side. She was in agony and he was sure the pain was getting worse despite the pain killer.

Jacob stood up and walked back to the control centre. When he was sat there earlier, he had noticed something that he was sure would be very useful. He found it now, nestled in a box under the desk – a sat phone. The mobile networks were down but this should work. He found Brady's number on the control centre and saved it into the sat phone then placed it carefully into his pocket where it nestled with the remaining inhalers. Then he searched on the computer for medical help. A long stream of names and numbers scrolled down in front of him working outwards from his exact location. The hospital he had just visited was top of course but he knew that there was nobody left there that could help. The morphine and bandages were great but only a temporary fix.

He started dialling using the computer network. This used the same technology as the sat phone and would always be the last network to go down. He dialled through doctor surgeries, through minor hospitals, even through vet surgeries. With each number he rang, he felt a slight glimmer of hope and then it diminished as the ringing tone went on and on. He imagined the telephones all over Melbourne ringing in offices, in doctors surgeries, in people's homes with no-one to answer it. He shuddered when he tried too hard to imagine the scene. Mutilated bodies in each house. He pictured a doctor's surgery full of patients that had turned into a bloodbath when two of the waiting patients and maybe a doctor had suddenly turned when they got the call – shedding their human faces to become the invading creatures and decimating the human flesh in the building.

He was reaching desperation point, keeping a scared eye on Rebecca, when he called Dr Martin Chase, MPA, BDC, and private GP apparently according to his website. He specialised in sporting injuries and lived in an exclusive part of Melbourne. He had a long list of celebrity clients and seemed to be very expensive to even have a consultation with let alone get treatment from.

Jacob wearily called his number and heard the normal constant ringing tone. He had got into a habit of letting the phone ring twenty times and then moving onto the next one. On the nineteenth ring, it was picked up. He could hear the connection; there was the unmistakable sound of someone breathing on the other end, just for a moment, and then it was slammed back down. Jacob almost fell off his chair. He rang back again instantly and heard it ring three times before it was picked up again.

"What do you want..?" said a very clear, very drunk Australian voice. "You shouldn't be ringing me, I'm off duty." He coughed now, a long rasping cough that eventually tailed off and then Jacob heard mutterings as if he had forgotten he was still connected to someone on the phone. Then in a louder voice that made Jacob jump: "I said, what do you want?".

"Sir, I need help. I realise you're off duty." Jacob felt stupid saying it – after all, wasn't everyone off duty now, but this man had clearly tried to forget what was going on in the outside world by drinking himself stupid. He wondered how he was still alive. "I need medical help though. Or rather, my friend does. She's hurt."

"Oh God, leave me alone please. My head hurts. Make an appointment with ....with someone and come and see me in a month". He laughed to himself, a long dry laugh. "Oh whatever, come on over. I don't care anymore."

Jacob thanked him, checked the address and was about to put the phone down when Dr Chase added: "And bring a bottle. It's a bring a bottle party!"

CHAPTER TWENTY EIGHT

They met no creatures on the way to Barry's car. Jacob's mental connection had gone now but he was sure they couldn't have repopulated the area that fast. That's not to say that there weren't other aliens that had answered some kind of distress call and hurried on over. They had to be quick though. Jacob was carrying Rebecca in his arms; her cheek nestled against his shoulder and the warmth of her body against his. He opened the front door with one hand and gently placed her in the passenger side taking care not to knock her wound. She was semi unconscious now, her eyes glazed. He buckled her in and got into the driver's side, turned the key to start the engine and drove out of the car park.

He had printed out a map showing the way to the doctors house and was grateful to see it was only two miles away; that should take them about five minutes. He turned on to the main road and drove carefully; he was still wary of creatures appearing from buildings and also careful to avoid any bumps in the road.

He was steering slowly around a car that had been abandoned in the middle of the road when a shadow passed over his car. A space craft was hovering in front of his car – not one of the huge ones he had entered before; this looked like some kind of reconnaissance craft. Jacob gritted his teeth and jammed his foot down on the accelerator. He felt the tyres spin on the road, the vehicle fishtailed for a moment and then thankfully it shot forward. The craft above him fired a white beam and it smashed into the road where the car had been moments earlier. Tarmac and dust flew up from the road and Jacob saw a small crater in his rear view mirror. He had not gone through all of this and found a way to fight back just to have it finish like this.

'When will it end?' he thought to himself. He kept his speed up, trying to avoid obstacles in the road as well as checking his mirrors for signs of the craft behind him. Rebecca was being thrown around much too much for his liking and she moaned gently in pain.

He saw it again coming from his right this time and he wrenched the wheel left to swerve into a side street. He was still going in the right direction for the doctors as far as he could tell but how was he going to get rid of this thing? It buzzed behind him and Jacob saw with alarm that the weapon on the bottom of the craft was beginning to glow red –getting ready to fire? He slammed on the brakes and Rebecca cried out as she jerked forward in the seat, her seatbelt holding her safe but pressing onto her wound. The craft flew onwards while Jacob threw the car in reverse spinning the wheel so that the car turned back to the direction it had been going.

He slammed down on the accelerator again and they were off, swerving again around obstacles and eating up the distance between them and the doctors. All of a sudden Jacob realised that they couldn't get to the doctors house with this thing in tow; that would lead them all to certain death. He tried to think of a way to lose it. He could see it now buzzing behind him, swooping low to keep track of the small speeding car.

 To his right, he noticed a sign for a multi-storey car park. 'Perfect' he thought. He waited until the last possible moment and then swung the steering wheel to the side and slammed on the brakes. The car slid, tyres squealing, the smell of burning rubber filling the air. Jacob then pressed the throttle once more and it shot up a small ramp, crashing through a wooden barrier and into the car park. Rebecca wasn't making any sound anymore and he was getting desperately worried about her. He needed to lose this thing fast. Looking behind him whilst advancing into the car park, he could see it buzzing outside the entrance in frustration – it was too big to get in.

Jacob began to look for the exit, hoping it was on the other side of the car park but slammed his fist on the steering wheel as he noticed the entrance was also the exit. He turned the car round instead and began to head up the ramp to the next level. Up and up he went until he finally reached the 12th floor just below the roof.

He came to a halt in the middle of the gloomy car park and got out of the car. There was no time to lose. He ran to the edge and carefully peered over. It was as he had hoped – the reconnaissance ship was also making its way up the levels outside the structure. It was weaving from left to right trying to see inside the car park and identify its prey. Jacob looked wildly around him. He spotted what he needed twenty feet away and ran over, checking over his shoulder when he got there just to make sure it hadn't found them yet.

In the corner, next to the door leading down to the staircase was a breeze block. His original plan had been to use a bin but this would do perfectly. He didn't know how it had got there and right now he really didn't care. He picked it up and staggered to the side – this thing was heavy. Peering over the side again, he saw the craft still below him, two levels down. It was still weaving from side to side and his aim was going to have to be perfect.

He balanced it on the barrier, said a little prayer, waited until it was weaving back towards the middle and then dropped it off the side. He couldn't have asked for a better shot. The breeze block landed straight on top of the craft, in the middle of its body. It let out a plume of black smoke and plummeted to the ground landing in a pile of twisted metal. Jacob lay his head on the cool barrier and breathed a sigh of relief. He turned, looked back at Rebecca slumped in the car and ran back to her. Getting into the drivers side, he started the ignition once more and headed back out of the car park.

It took him another two or three minutes to figure out where he now was as he strayed from his route marked on the map but he eventually got back on track and pulled up at the doctors a few minutes later.

Dr Chase lived in a high walled gated building with a security camera. Jacob rolled up to the gate and flashed his lights so the camera could see him. When this didn't work, he beeped his horn and waited. He didn't want to get out of the car and leave Rebecca in her vulnerable state. After a short while, there was a buzz, a click and the gate slowly drew back allowing him to drive in and make his way up the long winding drive to the house. Despite the situation, Jacob couldn't help but be impressed by the house. It was futuristic without looking strange. It was made of glinting metal and glass and the main lounge seemed to join seamlessly into the giant swimming pool. The beautifully kept lawn swept down and out of sight.

As he parked his car by the front door and got out, a man came out of the door, looking unsteady on his feet and with a stupid grin plastered on his face. The smell of alcohol hung around him like an invisible cloud.

"Doctor Chase, I presume?" Jacob said.

"Ah. My 2pm appointment." He smiled at Jacob and held his hands out wide, nearly falling over with the sudden movement. "You're late I'm afraid. While I was waiting, the whole world ended. Careless." He started wagging a finger at Jacob in admonishment.

"Doctor Chase. It's my friend. Please can you help? She's been shot and she's not moving anymore. Doctor?"

The man stood up straight and rubbed two fists in his eyes. Then he slapped himself across the cheeks twice leaving red hand marks on his cheeks. When he looked again at Jacob, he could see a glimpse of the doctor that practised before the invasion.

"Of course", Doctor Chase said, "come through."

Jacob opened Rebecca's door and carried her behind the doctor who led them into his surgery. He indicated that Jacob should lay her down on his table then stood next to her looking down at Rebecca.

"Beautiful girl. Beautiful girl. Well done." He nodded at Jacob who was glaring at him. He shook his head and squinted at him, muttering an apology. "Okay, what have we got?"

Jacob had half a mind to walk out but to where? He watched as Dr Chase unwound the bandage that he had put on earlier. Blood oozed from her wound and he asked Jacob to hold dressing pads underneath to soak up the blood. He seemed to be getting into his stride now – to be working on autopilot.

After examining her thoroughly, he smiled at Jacob.

"She's going to be fine. The bullet has passed through. There is an exit wound on the back which is good news. As far as I can see, it has caused no lasting damage and I can sew these wounds up."

Jacob collapsed in the chair behind him.

"Thank you. Oh God, thank you." He said. "Are you sure? She's still unconscious."

"I'm sure" Doctor Chase said. "I may be drunk as a lord but I know my stuff mate. She's going to be okay. And I'm pretty sure she's out for the count because you gave her enough morphine to stun a horse but that's fine too. She needs a good sleep after all she's been through. Let's move to somewhere comfortable and then I'll get you a drink."

"Thanks Doctor, but I really need to talk to someone first. Let's get her onto that sofa."

Supporting her limp body between them, they lay Rebecca onto the sofa. Jacob got out his sat phone and his heart leapt with joy to see the strong signal bars staring back at him.

He dialled the number for Chief Brady and heard the clear welcoming sound of a ringing tone in his ear.

Chief Alfred Brady was in a meeting with his department heads when his secretary knocked on the door. Even with murderous aliens at the gate, politeness was key and manners cost nothing. Brady beckoned her in.

"Sir, there's a telephone call for you. I think you're going to want to take this right now."

"Who is it?"

"It's Jacob Brooks, Sir. Calling from Australia."

Jacob. He'd assumed that he was dead after seeing the chaos break out on the television show and, despite their previous bad feeling, his grim mood was lifted by the news. He turned to his telephone, saw the green light blinking and pressed it to connect the call. He then pressed the speakerphone button so that the room could hear.

"Jacob?"

"Chief Brady Sir. Thank God you're still there. How is the infestation back home?" Jacobs voice echoed round the office loud and clear from the other side of the planet.

"It's bad. We've lost about thirty percent of our staff one way or another but that's minimal losses compared to the rest of the country. We've been tracking communications and linking up with pockets of useful sites across the country but things are breaking up fast. These things infiltrated us so well, damn it."

"Don't I know it" said Jacob.

Brady knew he was making a point; that if he had listened to him, things may have been different. But would they really? Wasn't it always going to end up like this?

"The government is still functioning although on a limited basis, there are areas of the country that the military are still holding but it's like a warzone. The television is down, the main radio networks are still down.

I've got the staff working on ways to help with the war effort here. We've got about twenty creatures outside the gate trying to get in but we're holding them off for now with makeshift flame throwers connected to the main gas line. It's incredibly risky but it seems to hold them back. Not kill them, I have no idea how to do that yet."

"That's why I'm ringing Sir. I think I've found a way."

Brady sat bolt upright in his chair. The four other heads of department in his office looked up with tired eyes and all stared at the telephone.

"Go on", said Brady slowly.

Jacob ran through his experiences in the last few hours – the small boy in the hospital, the asthma inhaler, the ship, the mental connections. It took him around ten minutes to go through it all and when he's finished, the room in England was quiet.

Brady slammed his hand down on the desk hard and they all jumped in their seats. In one movement, he span round in his chair and stood up, walking briskly to the window. He looked out at the creatures at the gate.

"We're going to get you, you little..." he muttered under his breath.

CHAPTER TWENTY NINE

In his mind, Jacob had expected a sweeping victory. The mixture of chemical would be produced by the lorry load. Firemen would fill their engines with it and hose it over the aliens. Aeroplanes would be loaded with it and they would spray it over the cities killing every last creature in sight. They would twist and burn in the streets, the human race would dance on their foaming bodies and reclaim the Earth.

The reality, of course, was somewhat different. The factories that made the chemicals were deserted; their workers either hiding at home somewhere or dead. It was the same with the firemen and the pilots.

That one phone call did change the world, however.

Chief Alfred Brady had been communicating with anyone and everyone that could possibly help. He had a team of scientists at his disposal that either worked on a solution or died at the hands of the creatures outside. More importantly, he had spoken to a chemicals plant in York that were in the same situation as them. They had forty workers hemmed in by aliens – they were keeping them out by barricading themselves inside. After realising they had access to two out of the three chemicals needed, Brady's scientists managed to find an alternative to the third using computer simulations with the other chemicals in the factory.

After a couple of trials, they thought they had as close as they were going to get and did a high tech experiment by throwing a bucket of the mixture out of the window onto the aliens below. A group of three had gathered by the side wall and were trying to dig their way through the bricks. The mixture landed in-between all three splattering the mixture over all of them. It wasn't as dramatic as Jacob's inhaler but it did the job. They wheeled away screaming in that high pitched squeal. Falling to their knees, then onto their stomachs, they burned slowly seemingly from the inside out. It took ten minutes for their bodies to foam away completely but they were incapacitated straight away.

Encouraged by this, they refined the chemical and cleared their area the next day. However, they were running out of the chemical fast. Brady stepped back in and found more supplies dotted across the country. Then he found volunteers to take massive risks and find whatever transport they could find to get the chemicals to each other and get the mix right. Hundreds of people died in this mission and the creatures knew what they were doing - they started blockading the factories and attacking the workers.

Brady and Jacob transmitted the weapon to the world. A large shipment, already mixed, was located in Paraguay and used to clear the capital city of aliens. The process of this one simple act took the lives of 650 men and women from the local towns and 3000 aliens.

Jacobs discovery and subsequent phone call changed the future of the planet. The human race was less than a week from being wiped off the planet and recolonised. It was now the battleground for a world war. Humans were fighting back. Soldiers dipped their bullets in the mixture. Gradually, they gained ground. But the war continued.

Three months after the phone call, Brady called the Melbourne Space and Science Centre for the daily update.

The new Centre Head answered promptly.

"Jacob Brooks speaking."

"Jacob, it's Alfred. How are things?"

Things were good. Brady had offered to fly Jacob and Rebecca back to work with him again in Exeter but they had refused for two reasons. Firstly, there was no way either of them were going to get on a plane again. Secondly, they were starting a new life here together. They had decided to take over control of the Centre in Melbourne to carry on and honour Barry's work.

They had found a beautiful house on the beach that had been vacated by an unlucky family at the start of the war. It sounded idyllic and in another situation it would have been, but they lived with four other people. They all took it in shifts to guard the house and doused the aliens in the limited mixture they had. So far they had survived but they never knew how long that success would last. Jacob and Rebecca were happy and they knew that as long as they were together, they could take whatever the aliens could throw at them. They had love and science on their sides and that was a potent mixture.

Three miles above the Earth, the giant craft continued to hover. The remaining occupants studied, analysed and finally decided on the best way to wipe the vermin from the face of the planet.

The Second Wave was due to begin.

THE END

Made in the USA
Charleston, SC
17 June 2014